Blood Runs Deep

Tommie Harvey

Contents

Chapter 1

"**Y**our turn, son."

I don't bother offering any sort of acknowledgment, too focused on the ring in front of me. Too focused on my opponent and what I know is about to happen. Part of me feels sick but part of me knows this is the way it has to be. It's all about survival so I cannot afford petty emotions of any kind. It is time to shut down and do what I need to fucking do.

Boisterous cheers and deep calls of encouragement meet my eardrums as soon as I step into the ring. I know a lot of them are only because I am the son of Abram and they fear me. Only a small portion cheer because they know how far my skills and talents go. Son of Abram or not, I am a protégé of destruction. That's how I earned the name that's bouncing off the four walls of this dark warehouse.

"Raze! Raze! Raze!"

Raze. To destroy. To completely eliminate.

I was conditioned to annihilate. My opponent does not know that or he wouldn't be stepping into the ring with me, especially not with that smug fucking smirk. If he knew what was good for him he would turn around and get out of here while that was still an option. Instead, his shoulders are loose and his expression relaxed.

He thinks he is just fighting some twenty-two year old punk. He has no idea it is the last thing he'll ever do.

I feel numb inside. I've shut myself off completely. It's the only way to see this through. My eyes are hard and unblinking and my opponent eagerly circles me. He's eating up the attention and bouncing on his feet like a fucking child. He should be ashamed of himself. I stay perfectly still in my corner of the ring. Not because I am scared or nervous by any means—but because I know how easy this will be. This will be over before it has the chance to begin.

"You're prepared?" Father asks in my ear.

"You should know better than to ask me that," I respond flatly. After all, he is the one who trained me. If you train at the hands of Abram since before you could even walk, as I have, than the outcome of the match is all too clear.

Father scoffs but I know it's to conceal smug laughter. He knows as well as I do that I am just as good a fighter he is. Better even, though we both pretend that's not the case. Ego is all a man has sometimes.

"This is your only chance," He reminds me as if he hasn't been chanting the same fucking thing for years now. "This is where you prove yourself. If you are to be the youngest gang leader this city has ever witnessed, you must leave no room for doubt. Is that clear?"

If he wants me to be the leader so badly, why not simply trust in my abilities as I do? It's a response he wouldn't appreciate so I settle on a disinterested, "Yes."

"Good."

There is no praise in it. It's just a word spoken for the sake of response. In all my years I have never been praised and I don't expect to be. I don't expect anything from anyone. I wouldn't be the machine I am if I did. I would be human, which is something I can't afford in the life I've been brought into. If I was human, I would have regrets. If I had regrets, I would drown under the weight of them. It is a matter of survival and that means no one can stand in my way or they get taken down too.

"You're familiar with the rules." Byron's commanding voice overtakes the noise and a hush falls around us. As my father's right-hand man, he is just as feared as Abram himself. Not exactly the same but enough that we all are wise enough not to cross him. "You select a weapon of choice. You fight. Only one man leaves the ring breathing. Proceed."

Two henchman step inside holding a selection of weapons. My opponent chooses a flail—a metal rod with a spiked ball attached at the end. What he hopes to achieve with that is futile because he won't have the chance to wield it if he's fighting me. He smirks like I should be afraid, when he should only be worried about himself. I don't so much as glance at him as I grab the brass knuckles and fit them on to my hand. The brass have little protruding spikes in them that, although small, cut deep and clean. It's not the most effective weapon but if you can fight with skill and precision, it is deadly. Maybe that's why my opponent guffaws at me. He really is ignorant and it makes any semblance of guilt I might have had evaporate. He should be humble if he expects mercy and now, he won't receive any.

The cheers resume when Byron steps out of the ring. Any minute now he will call for us to begin. I pull in a deep breath through my nose to relax my muscles. I flex my fighting hand to loosen it and open my legs for better stance.

Fighting is in my nature. I would say second nature but it's instilled much deeper than that. Fighting is what I am made of so here, in this ring, feels like home. This is where I belong. This is what I was born to do. It's why I'm not nervous or anxious for what is about to happen. I'm too agile to lose my upper hand, too skilled to lose, and too cold to be afraid. This will only take a matter of seconds.

"Begin!" Byron commands.

Roars thunder around the warehouse and rattle the walls. The men have gone ballistic with testosterone and anticipation. They are ready for the fight they were promised—the fight to see who will be the next leader of the South Bloods.

My opponent was the only man stupid enough to claim he should be leader. The title has always been mine but he underestimates me. He mistakes me for a child, and I will defeat him and make him less of a man for it.

He swings his flail, the spiked ball whipping through the air and cutting the atmosphere in half. Idiot. He stumbles forward with the weight as I predicted and he's now close enough for me to reach him. It's a mere second, if that, where he glances up to meet my eyes. His are afraid, pooling with the realization of his grave mistake, and mine are void of any emotion. He has only himself to blame.

My hand grips his shoulder as he keels over me. His frame, slightly taller than mine, bends to eye-level. I keep mine latched onto his and my other arm whips up so the brass knuckles connect with his throat. His mouth falls open and fails to pull in the oxygen he was hoping to gather. My stare is unblinking as I yank the spikes out of his throat, not even registering the splatter of blood that shoots all over my chest and face. He falls to his knees, mouth open and desperately clawing at air. Blood flows out of him in large spurts and colours the white canvas beneath us. In seconds his eyes roll to the back of his head until only the whites are visible and his body crumples to the ground. Dead. Ten seconds into our fight.

Nobody is shocked. We all knew this man had a death wish the moment he thought he could fight me for my throne. There is not even a second to mourn for his lifeless body, even as blood continues to seep out of him and drain him of his soul. The cheering intensifies as men smack the walls and floors and howl into the night. The warehouse fills up with the sound of victory and the stench of death. I feel none of it.

"It is done!" Father bellows. He enters the ring and raises my fist to the air. Vicious roars greet me. I keep my jaw locked and my eyes vacant. They will fear me from this moment on. "Bow to your new leader!"

Chapter 2

7 years later...

My knuckles meet flesh and a crack sounds into the night, followed by a whimper of pain. Pathetic. I take hold of a head and bring it down on my knee with brute force. More whimpers as the body falls to the floor.

"Please," Lloyd croaks. "M-mercy."

"You are begging?" I sneer. "South Bloods do not beg! Get on your feet."

He scrambles, raising himself on his feet with strained effort. The brick wall of the dark alleyway holds him up because his body cannot. He leans against it and his harsh, pained breaths are the only sounds among the hushed night we are surrounded in.

"Who is responsible?" I ask again. "Do not lie to me. It wouldn't please me to kill you but if that's what must be done, that will be your fate. You decide."

"I have a family," He whispers. "You know that."

"And you know my rules." I don't miss a beat. "In my kingdom, you follow them. So tell me—who. Is. Responsible?"

"I don't know."

"This is a lie."

"I swear on our people, I don't!"

"How dare you?" I grab him by the collar of his shirt and slam him back against the wall. He groans in agony. "You swear on our people? The very people you failed to protect? I think you wish to die, Lloyd."

"I don't know what happened," He bites out. "Raze, please—"

My fingers lock around his throat and his eyes protrude. His fight for oxygen is one he will fail if I don't get answers. "That does not save you! Not knowing what happened is worse. It was your duty to watch our men. Who the fuck killed our men?"

I loosen my fingers just enough so that he can speak. His face contorts in anger and he strikes his leg out to nail my stomach. I release him, not because he caught me by surprise, but because I will allow him a final chance to stand his ground before I'm through with him. As I've said, ego is all a man has sometimes. I will allow him to go down with honour even if he's undeserving.

"Fuck you!" He spits. He puffs his chest out with false courage. He thinks he claimed the upper hand, that he rivalled me in strength. It's making him drunk with power. His lip curls as he gets into my space and shoves me back by the chest. Again, I allow him. My men go for their weapons but I hold a hand out to ward them off. "You know what your problem is? You're fucking spoiled. Just because Abram created this gang doesn't mean you're fit to run it as his son. I keep telling you I don't know how the ambush happened! If you were a true leader you would believe me!"

His fists clench like he's ready to...what? Fight me? I tilt my head just barely. What a horrible idea for him to consider.

"I never liked your smug ass," I click my tongue.

Lloyd flinches as I go for my pocket, all the more evidence that he is a coward, but forces himself to relax when I pull out a mere recording device. He's confused until I play the tape. His face drains of blood when he recognizes his voice.

"They're protecting the shipment on the warehouse just outside of Buffalo. It's five men including me so bring at least ten. Wait for my signal before you start shooting. Last fucking thing we need is for me to get caught in the crossfire. And bring the money I asked for or the deal is off."

I shut off the recording and Lloyd backs up, eyes darting for a way out. He won't find one.

"Which gang did you cut this deal with?" I demand in a low voice. "Speak the truth or the next minutes of your life will be excruciatingly painful."

"You don't understand," He pleads. "I was low on money. I was desperate."

"You are a traitor." I take a step forward and he backs up into the wall, trapped. "We look after our own. You were to approach me for a loan if you needed cash. Instead, four of our men are dead because of your greed. This is the last I will ask of you—who is responsible for their deaths?"

His mouth pinches into a thin line. He would rather protect the killers than himself? Then he should expect nothing less than death.

"Raze." He eyes the knife in my hand with a sort of maniacal frenzy. "You can't do this."

"Now you decide what I can and can't do?" I shake my head pitifully. "Your next words dictate what will be made of you. I am out of patience. Answer your leader, now."

"Fine!" His knees knock together and I glance down just as the front of his jeans darken in colour. I sneer. Disgusting man. "It was the Asesinos! I give you my word!"

"Your words mean nothing." I poise the tip of my knife at his jugular. He doesn't dare move. "What business did they want with the South Bloods?"

"T-they're looking to expand. They want to be as high-profile as we are. They've been stealing drugs and heavy artillery from all kinds of gangs and selling them for double the price."

"They will fail, just as you have."

"Raze, no! Please!"

The tip of the knife digs into his skin and just barely breaks the surface. A dot of blood appears and Lloyd gulps down bursts of air. His eyes are full of desperation and they plead with me. Stupid, stupid man. He was safe with us. He knows better than to make himself an enemy, especially to me. Part of me wants to spare the man I've known for a decade but I cannot make this decision with emotions. As a leader, I cannot show even an ounce of weakness for the sake of credibility alone. He shouldn't have expected mercy. He did this to himself.

"Run," I command. "While you can."

A man should die with hope. He should die believing he has a chance. Lloyd's eyes widen but he wastes no time taking off, his feet pounding heavily on the cement.

I count to three before I propel forward and follow him. I'm faster, more agile, and level-headed. His panic has made it impossible for him to breathe steady so he is breathless seconds into his run. I catch him by the back of his shirt and yank, wrapping my arm around his chest to lock him in place. He screams, begs, but it's pointless. I raise my hand and slash the knife across his throat, letting go of his body. It falls to the ground with a lifeless thump and he bleeds out all over the pavement. I wipe my knife on the back of his shirt and straighten up again.

"Get rid of it," I say when my men catch up. "I don't want any questions."

"What now?" One of them asks. The rest gather Lloyd's corpse and make calls for the tools to dispose of him.

"We avenge our men." I stick the knife back in my pocket and head for my car, knowing the rest will follow. "This is the final time any gang will cross me."

Or it will be my body bleeding out.

Chapter 3

My father paces the length of his study. He is not worried. Nothing shakes him. He is furious and I am the culprit.

I stand tall with my hands behind my back. At almost thirty-years-old, he manages to make me feel like an incapable child. It makes me resent him more than I already do. I never wanted this life but I owned up to it and I do it well. He should not ask more of me. He already owns my soul.

"A mess!" He hisses. "Have you learned nothing at all?"

"It was taken care of quietly and efficiently," I rebuke calmly. Inside, a storm rages. "You are exaggerating."

He stops mid-stride and turns his gaze on me, eyes narrowed. "Watch your mouth, boy."

Watch your back, old man.

I say nothing, though I burn to.

He resumes his pacing with a scowl. "Twelve Asesinos are dead. Who do you think they will blame? They know it was the doing of the South Bloods."

I shrug. "We all know it. We also know they killed our men first. What was I to do—let them walk away?"

"This will start a rivalry. A feud. Then what do you suggest?"

"We deal with it accordingly. No one is starting anything for the time being. They received the message."

"What made them think they could make the first move in the first place? Don't they fear you? Their actions suggest they don't."

I pull in a slow breath before I do something idiotic like take a swing at him. He's being petty. Childish. In almost eight years of running this gang, I have raised it to its true potential. We have fewer enemies, more allies, and are more organized in our distribution. There's no need to be ruthless unless someone makes the first move. The South Bloods are thriving. We're at the top of the food chain. I've outdone the mighty Abram and he cannot stand it. He's trying to pick me apart and look for mistakes in plain sight. He's losing his touch.

"They fear me just fine," My jaw ticks. "This is the first any man has attempted to betray me."

"And why is that? What provoked him to do such a thing?"

"It had nothing to do with me. It was his own greed and it blinded him from what mattered. He made a mistake because he was human." And I hate that I had to take his life for it.

Father pauses like he knows what I'm thinking. My shoulders tighten defensively when his eyes narrow on me. "Just what are you implying? That he deserved to live?" He spits the word out like poison.

"No," I lie. "He made his choice. It was the first and last time anyone will cross me. The Asesinos are now in our debt. Unless they want to dig their grave deeper they won't attempt anything like that again. If they do, we'll be ready."

"I don't like this." Of course he doesn't. "A feud does not bode well for us."

"Why? Gang rivalry is common. The Asesinos dropped the ball first and that's out of our control. We can either deal with it or cower. I'm not afraid if they decide to take this further. I trust my ability to handle it, as should you."

This time I've talked out of my ass. I'm too fired up to care. Father stalks right up to me until we're nose-to-nose and his harsh breathing fans my face. I don't so much as blink.

"Do not even think about suggesting that I'm afraid. I don't give a fuck about a rivalry because I know I'd win. I'm just not sure you would, boy."

"I would." The urge to smirk is strong but I stop myself. "And if it comes down to it, I will. I fear nothing. You know this."

The first thing he ever taught me was to never show weakness. I was to trust in myself with unshakable confidence. Nothing makes another person more uncomfortable than knowing they can't get through to you. It makes them feel beneath you because they can't measure up to the level you've established. My father cannot stand the irony that I've used this strategy on him. In this moment he is not my equal because I didn't allow him to get under my skin for even a second. It only draws attention to how my leadership skills have profoundly outdone his. He wanted to create a leader as powerful as himself—instead, he created a protégé he cannot keep up with.

He locks his jaw with spite and turns away. I wait patiently as he mutters to himself and looks through a pile of papers, sighing deeply.

"Damage control," He barks. "You've drawn attention to yourself whether you like it or not. Flying under the radar is no longer an option. You need a front, an identity, something you can rely on when unwanted questions come your way."

"Already done," I say calmly and his head snaps up. "Byron campaigned me as an up and coming boxer. It is the most convenient cover and doable too. Running this gang means fewer fights and I don't want to lose my touch just because I'm caught up in business. It will also explain the injuries I'm usually covered in and my large source of income. Fighters make a lot of money professionally."

"Byron didn't mention anything." I don't miss the accusation in his voice.

"There was no need. We have it under control."

"His loyalties are to me before they are to you," Father rebukes in an acidic tone. "You are not to leave me out of any discussions or go above my head ever again. Is that understood?"

He is a blind man. If he opened his eyes just once, he would see that treating his right-hand man like garbage is the reason Byron prefers me to him. He is a good partner. I think of him as my equal, unlike my father.

"Understood," I say instead.

"Explain this boxing angle. I fail to see how it would be of any service if fighting professionally puts you under a spotlight."

"I'm no longer under the radar. You've said it yourself. I'm recognized too easily on these streets so it should be for something good, something the public won't fear. Professional boxing requires the skills I already possess. It will serve as training between business so I don't lose my combat abilities. The pay will support running this gang. Most importantly, a steady occupation helps me blend in. I can't chalk up my wealth to inheritance much longer. The government is getting suspicious. We both knew I'd have to come up with an identity at some point."

"Boxing of all things?"

"It will work," I stress. "I've already been campaigned. My exhibition match is in a week and I will work my way up into the industry."

"You have to win every match for this to be the case."

This time I don't bother hiding my annoyance. "I've never lost a match. Boxing is child's play to what I've trained for all my life. The men that face me will lose every time."

He leans back in his chair, breathing through his nose. "Yes. That much is true, at least. But they don't allow killing in this profession?"

"No killing," I confirm. "Clean-cut rules and several ways to win."

"Shame," Father mutters. "No point in watching if there's no death."

Sick man. My nostrils flare with disapproval but he's too caught up in his head to notice.

"Fine," He relents. "Have your fun. But remember this is only meant to serve as a cover. A false identity. It's not who you really are. You are the leader of the South Bloods and a ruthless killer. Your duty to this family comes before anything else. If you fail to recognize that, I'm not responsible for what will be made of your betrayal."

He means he doesn't care if I have to die for choosing anything beyond this family. My father would rather I die for my loyalties, than live on as a traitor. Sick, sick man.

"Is that all?" My tone is unwavering. I've long since learned to detach myself from petty emotions like hurt or love. They are the worst things a human can feel.

"Dismissed," He waves me off without another glance.

I stalk out of his study and head for my own office instead. I know my duty is to this life but it doesn't mean I don't hate every fucking second of it.

Chapter 4

1 year later...

"Ready?" My partner, Mitch, asks in a low tone.

He is new to South Bloods. My age but it's obvious he didn't belong. Got roped up into some shit and found his way in the middle of the most ruthless gang in New York. He was scared shitless the first night he was shoved forward to meet me and present his intentions. He held his own, jaw raised in courage. Not defiance. It was a trait I appreciated and I took him under my wing immediately. I will always be a killer, but at least I can choose to protect some. He's since proved to be useful as I knew he would. He understands my logic and the way I do things so he works completely on par with me. It's a good match.

"Always," I smirk a little and he tosses one back. I'll also always be a leader, but with Mitch around sometimes I pretend I can be a regular asshole with no responsibilities. I allow myself to loosen up for some moments.

He pats my shoulder. "Go easy on the guy."

"That, I can't promise." I stuff both my hands into the red gloves while eyeing my opponent. He stares back at me warily.

In the year since my exhibition match, I made a name for myself quicker than anticipated. I knew I would outdo the fighters I faced with ease but I didn't think I'd face next to no challenges. Some fighters are good and show potential, but they are all stiff and hold back. I was taught never to hold back so I have a level of control they don't. I can push my limits and draw back easily. These fighters don't even know what their limits are and their self-doubt is something I take advantage of every time.

True to my confident declaration that day in the study, I've not yet lost a fight. It's almost too easy. I haven't so much as taken a hit. It's more like training than fighting to me but that's partially why I did this so I keep up with it. The money is reliable, increasing with each fight I win, and dealing with the government and their suspicions is no longer a bitch. To the world, I'm professional boxer Greg Resnick. Those who know the truth know me as Raze, the cold killer.

Admittedly, I prefer Greg to Raze but I know that's not an option. After a year of doing this I've found myself growing attached to the mediocre lifestyle of a famous fighter. It's a death wish and one I have to reprimand myself for constantly. What am I going to do—leave the South Bloods? Ridiculous. I know better than that. I shouldn't even have such thoughts.

"You good?" Mitch asks and I realize I'm grinding my teeth.

I loosen myself up. I cannot show weakness or doubt. My eyes harden quickly. "Fine. Just have a lot to do after this match."

Which is true. I've been monitoring the Asesinos closely this past year. Things were quiet for a while there but I'm hearing rumours that I don't appreciate. If they try to make another move on the South Bloods, I will spare no one. My warnings are not to be taken lightly and if they are then I'm not responsible. I try to salvage life. These idiots are asking to have it taken away.

Mitch chucks me on the back in a friendly manner I'm not familiar with. I don't have any friends. I was too busy being fine-tuned to fight to make friends or create relations of any kind. It's a situation I don't know how to approach so I stay quiet instead, not offering any acknowledgement.

The referee motions for both fighters to move to the centre. I find it odd that a referee is required at all. When two men fight, it should be between them only. But rules are rules, I guess. And boxing is not meant to be ruthless. Oddly enough, I appreciate that. Killing is not something I want to do unless I have to and I forgot what it's like to fight just for the sport of it. I would say it's fun but that's ridiculous. This is just business. There is no room for fun.

The referee blows a whistle to signal the start of the match. My opponent circles me and bounces on his heels. If he feels the need to move this much then he's nervous. Otherwise he would be smart about it and reserve his energy, save the pent up adrenaline and wisely use it to fight instead of burning it away dancing. I suppress an agitated sigh. Who trains these amateurs? Training dictates what kind of fighter a man will be. These men have not been guided properly and won't put up a deserving fight. It's maddening, but none of my business.

My opponent won't stay still. My mouth twists down with irritation because he's giving away all his tells. He's wasting this time and allowing me to learn his fighting. By the time he actually makes a move, I'll see it coming. Doesn't he understand that?

When it's obvious he won't do anything expect bounce around, I make the first move. My arm shoots forward in a straight punch that knocks his chin back. There was enough force behind it that he staggers back and falls into the ropes. I'm not one to waste time so I'm on him immediately, drilling down with hook after hook as he struggles to remove himself. He's gone on defence, but he should know a man my size won't let up. The only way to get past me is through me but he's cowering. This match will go to me.

My gloves sinks into his eye socket and he cries out, eyes shut. Now he's not even looking at me. I bend on my knees and send body shots—chest, ribs, gut. He'll be bruised purple this time tomorrow. The force of my punches and the bursts of my breaths are all I hear against the roaring crowd. My focus is knocking him out so I can win this match and go about my business.

I make the mistake of glancing over his shoulder, out toward the crowd. I don't know what compels me. But even from my peripheral I could make out long hair amongst the bodies of big and burly men. The image sticks out like a sore thumb and I pause without meaning to.

It's a girl. Woman, really, but it doesn't make a difference because she looks like she shouldn't be here. Only men come to fights and on the rare occasion women come, they're usually tough and gritty themselves. This woman is not. She's very soft-looking. Fragile and small. She's also chewing her thumb nervously, as if it's her in the ring and not me. For a moment her eyes lock on mine and even with the measurable distance between us, I can tell how startling the shade of blue is.

And then she does the strangest thing—she smiles. It's a small, nervous, and sympathetic smile. All I can do is blink, breathing hard. In a room full of blood-thirsty men and overwhelming testosterone, this woman just smiled at me as if I deserve something as kind as that. My brows come together in confusion. A woman like that shouldn't be in a place like this. And she sure as hell shouldn't be smiling at me.

Suddenly my chin is knocked back so hard my teeth clatter together. It's so loud I can hear the way my mouth rattles but that could also be because a sudden hush falls over the arena. Aside from the surprised gasps, everyone has gone quiet as I stumble back and barely get hold of the ropes to keep myself upright. I blink again, more confused than ever.

That was the first time I've ever taken a hit in my life.

What the fuck just happened? Never, never, in all my years of fighting have I been hit or caught off guard like that. It's such a staggering realization that I simply stand in place and try to understand how I let this happen. I was distracted. I'm never distracted.

My opponent is brimming at the ass from false hope. He does that stupid fucking hop again and I can practically see his head increasing in size. I understand that he's the first man to get a hit on me but he cannot fight on adrenaline alone. He needs skill and precision and he lacks both. The next swing he takes only confirms that as I easily move out of the way. He straightens up, still smirking. No man should behave as if he's won until he has. Anything can happen in a fight.

I may have some sort of death wish because I glance out at the crowd again. The woman, she is leaving. I can't help but feel restless, a burning desire overtaking me at the thought of warning her not to come back. She shouldn't have been here in the first place. It's not my business but maybe it is, isn't it? She's here at my match and a woman like her shouldn't see these darker, uglier parts of life. She looked too good to be tainted by the evil we're surrounded in.

I waste no time. I press a glove into my opponent's chest to keep him in place and my other arm swings out. I punch with the force of ten men, a punch that is meant to injure gravely. The answering crack of his flesh tells me all I need to know before he even hits the ground. Still, I stand in the middle of the ring and humour the referee while he counts to ten to confirm the knockout. My opponent won't wake up for quite a while. The referee gets to ten and I take off immediately, ducking under the ropes.

"Holy shit," Mitch mumbles, falling into step with me. "I've never seen you get hit before. But man, you wasted no time putting him in place."

"Cover for me," I order instead of answering his observations. "Don't let anyone follow me. I need two minutes."

"For what?"

"Mitch." The warning in my eyes is clear. He knows better than to ask questions.

He nods, growing serious and getting back to business. "Do what you need to do."

I know he'll do as I asked. It's why I chose him for my partner. So I'm not worried as I duck away from the crowd's sight and toward the back exit where I saw her leave. I open the door and cool air hits my hot skin, charged up from the fight. I look around and squint against the dark, catching movement just ahead.

"Wait," I command. My deep voice carries across the parking lot and the woman jerks in obvious surprise. She stops and only then do I notice she's with someone.

"Holy crap," I hear the other girl mumble. "I think he's calling you."

"Come here," I beckon a finger. "Alone, please."

The word please sounds strange on my tongue. I don't think I've ever used it before and I have no idea why I used it now. It might have been the right call because the woman hesitantly heads for me, after her friend all but shoves her to move. Her steps are short and slow and her arms are pinned to her side. She thinks I haven't seen the keys she's clutching between her fingers. I'm impressed she thought to be prepared in the first place. I have good intentions but not everyone is like that. At least she knows that much.

I suck in a startled breath when the streetlight reveals her and I finally see her up close. She's...gorgeous. Possibly the most beautiful woman I've ever seen. Her face is full of soft features that make her endearing and inviting—sweet eyes, full lips, small button nose. Her hair is a wiry brown, a little plain but it suits her somehow. Her frame is staggeringly small. She's very tiny. Willowy and lithe, the barest of swells where they should be in a woman. But it's her hands that catch my attention. They're frail and covered in colourful paint. It's like she never bothered washing them. What a strange woman.

"Hi," She greets quietly. Even her voice is small and full of so much softness. "Are you okay?"

"What?" I feel the space between my brows crease. What on earth is she talking about?

"You were hurt," She says it like it's obvious. My expression doesn't shift so she tentatively reaches up. I have no idea what she's doing until her paint-stained hand brushes across my chin. My breath catches again when the contact sparks a zing up my spine. What the fuck is happening to me? "Right here."

Our eyes connect and for a moment I forget who I am. She looks at me like I intrigue her, a small and curious smile playing on those soft lips. Her head tilts and I'm taken aback that I find it almost adorable.

I catch her wrist swiftly and she gasps in surprise, baby blue eyes shifting to our joined hands. I don't know if it's because a strange man is touching her or maybe she feels that same zing I felt moments ago. I selfishly hope it's the latter, though I have no idea why I'm hoping at all.

"You don't belong here," I state.

At that her eyes come back to mine. This time she blinks, long lashes fluttering. "Um, why?"

"Women like you shouldn't be in places like this."

"Women like me?"

"Yes. You stick out in plain sight. The men that come to my matches are dangerous. If they take an interest in you, you can guarantee you'll be caught in something you shouldn't."

Her bottom lip juts out a little when she frowns. I've seen women pout when they try to be sexy and make a move. I don't think that's what this woman is doing. I don't think she needs to try anything to get attention.

"Thank you but I can take care of myself." The words are laced with a bit of annoyance. Again, I'm strangely impressed with her backbone.

I shake my head. "Not in a place like this. Don't come back."

Her mouth drops open with shock. She shouldn't do that around men. It's oddly enticing. "Um, no offence but you can't exactly tell me what to do."

"I can," I rebuke and cross my arms. Her eyes flit to my bare chest briefly before hastily moving away. "I have more influence in this city than you're aware of. Stay away from my matches."

Now she's very obviously pissed. She crosses her arms right back. "I was dragged here because my friends think I need to get out more but that's it. I wasn't going to come back anyways but now I really won't because wow, you're an ass."

"I'm aware." I fight the odd urge to smile at her haughty tone. Intuition tells me she isn't used to being riled up like this and the fact that I've achieved this is amusing. "So we've reached an agreement?"

She stares at me. "God, who are you?"

If she knows what's good for her, she won't ask again. I stay quiet instead of answering and this leads to a silent standoff of sorts. We do nothing but stare at each other and the tension gradually dissipates, replaced by curiosity once again. I feel like she's pulling me in somehow and I can't make sense of why. She searches my face like she knows exactly what I'm thinking. It's unnerving.

"Laura!" Her friends calls.

So that's her name. It suits her well. As sweet and innocent as she is.

She turns around and signals her friend to let her know she's coming instead of shouting back. I don't know why I'm noticing things like these. She faces me again and starts to back away, eyes holding mine.

"If anything, you look like you don't belong," She observes, her voice once again softer.

I humour her, only because I know I won't see her again. "What do you mean?"

She shrugs, chewing on the edge of her thumb nervously. "You look like you're struggling against yourself, like you're two people instead of one. You look like you're forced to be someone you're not."

I bristle. How could she know that? How could she see that in the two minutes I've spoken to her when no one else in my life has ever suspected as much? I can feel myself becoming defensive and my jaw locks.

"Don't come back," I warn her one last time. She's trouble. Too much fucking trouble based on how I've reacted to her tonight alone.

She nods like she expected that answer and, despite being upset with me, offers another smile. "Bye, Greg."

"It's Raze," I call back, annoyed, but she's already out of earshot as she rushes to her friend's side. It's been a long time since I've been Greg.

Chapter 5

I'm very annoyed. It might be because I haven't slept properly in a week. It might be because my father won't stop giving me shit for taking one fucking punch. It might be because the Asesinos are definitely planning something and I need to figure out what.

It might be because I'm still thinking about her. Laura.

Something about her completely undid me. Never mind the internal battle I was fighting in her proximity, but I stupidly blurted who I was before she walked away. Why did I tell her my name was Raze? The public was only supposed to know me by Greg. She is part of the public. Why did I offer the truth about myself? She can do anything with that information and I don't know her nearly well enough to guess what she might be up to. Maybe she doesn't care but maybe she looked into me and that poses a problem. A very large one.

I have to find her.

It's why I assigned Mitch with the task a couple of days ago. It's been a week since I saw her and I'm getting impatient. You can find out a lot about a person in one week, if she's interested enough that is. Again, I don't know her nearly well enough to say. And since Mitch is doing this for me solo it's taking longer than it normally would. He is the only one I trust to get this done. If anyone else in the South

Bloods discovered I'd taken an interest in this woman, she may as well be done for. I'm surprised at the surge of protectiveness that fills me at the thought.

Business as leader has kept me busy or I might have gone out of my mind by now. Taking care of shipments has been top priority since the ambush a year ago. Losing our men has brought us all on edge. Things are tense as I lead my team toward the docks to collect our latest cargo. Everyone is on high alert as we scope out our surroundings, our weapons in hand and ready for a fight. We will not be caught by surprise again.

I bring my fist up to signal them to stop and my men oblige. With hand gestures they've long since memorized, they follow my silent instructions to spread out. They take their assigned spots hiding behind the large crates and guns at the ready. I meet Byron's eye and he nods to let me know he has me covered.

With my gun tucked in the front of my jeans, I loosen my tense shoulders and make my way to the walkway where the boat is docked. I'm on edge, but the Vice Lords can't see that. We've never done business with them before but they had something the South Bloods have been looking for so it's a risk I had to take. My men are prepared regardless.

"Mike?" I call out the leader by name when I reach the boat. It's small in size so it doesn't take long to spot him rounding the corner, box in hand. A woman is with him and she holds a second box. I bend down to hold the boat by the edge while they step off to balance the weight and straighten up as they set the boxes down. "That's everything?"

"It is," Mike confirms. He points to the woman. "This is my wife, Nora."

I tip my chin. I don't give a fuck but clean business is the best business so I offer my respect. I dismiss them both just as quick as I crouch down, retrieving my knife from my boot to open the box.

"Woah," Mike waves a hand. "There's no need for that. It's all in there, boss."

I don't so much as blink. "Then you wouldn't mind me checking."

He must see the threat in my eyes because he takes a step back and gestures for me to go on. He doesn't look like the kind of man cut out for this life. He's too...pretty. And he won't stop scratching his arms so it doesn't take a genius to guess he's an addict. Probably some punk that got a taste of this life and thinks he's fit to be a leader now. I'm not impressed and I already know I won't be doing business with them again.

I get the box open and it reveals several packets stuffed to the hilt. I whistle with my teeth and Byron comes out from behind one of the crates, gun visible in hand.

Mike scowls. "There's no need for that."

"I don't wish to use it," I say without sparing him a glance. "Shut up before you give me a reason to."

He wisely stays quiet. Byron crouches down next to me to inspect the contents of the packaging, running a finger through the powder of a bag I ripped open. He's done this part longer than I have so I leave it up to him.

"Well?" I ask quietly.

"Authentic," He confirms. He lowers his voice too and turns his body toward mine. "Hell of an amount. Where'd they get it if they're a charity case?"

"My question exactly." We both look at Mike who's shuffling from foot to foot. "How did you pay for all of this?"

"Money," He smarts. Idiot. I take my gun out and point it at him. Nora screams and cowers behind him and Mike holds his hands up. "Hey, relax! Chill!"

"How did you pay for all of this?" I repeat, clicking back the lock.

He pales and I know he will take this more seriously. "A loan."

"From?"

"The Asesinos."

Byron and I share a grim look. I should not be surprised. Their plan is all too obvious now that I have the missing pieces to put in place. Give a loan to a low-profile gang and let them do the dirty work with shipments. Sell the cargo to a high-profile gang. If Mike and Nora are unable to pay them back and in the allotted time frame they were given, they can pin the owed money on us and have a reason to open fire. It would have been a smart plan if they didn't choose idiots to complete this job.

"No deal." I kick the box over to Mike, trying to conceal my anger. The Asesinos almost got away with it. This is too close for comfort. This is revenge.

"What the fuck?" Mike barks. "I brought this for our deal and now you won't pay me? What do I do now?"

"Your problem. Not mine." I gesture at Byron and we head off the docks. Mike looks like he wants to say something else until I point the gun at him, my face contorting with spite. "Don't reach out to me again. Consider it war if you come near the South Bloods. I'll kill you myself."

I don't wait for him to agree. If he knows what's good for him he won't try otherwise. I'm in a shitty mood as we head back toward our truck. Now I have to explain to father that this was nothing more than a bust. I'm ready to rip some heads off until I get a text alert and open up my phone, reading the new message.

Mitch: Found her.

The address is for a paint studio. I'm not surprised. I specifically asked Mitch to cross-reference her name with painters in the city and figured it would lead me to her.

I step out of the car, my eyes tracing the small building. I've seen apartments bigger than this studio. Either this woman is not talented or she just hasn't been recognized for her efforts yet. Something tells me it's the latter.

I ignore the closed sign and knock on the glass door. A few seconds tick by but I'm impatient after the day I've just had so I knock again, much harder than before. She finally comes into view and her blue eyes widen with shock when she sees me through the glass. I frown as I look over her. She's dressed in short overalls that expose her bare legs and they're covered in paint, like the rest of her. There's smatterings of red and black and grey all over her face, hair, and body. She's like a toddler.

I can tell she does not want to let me inside. She simply stands in front of the door while nervously eyeing me and shifting her weight. I point to the door handle, a silent demand to be let in. Her eyes graze over me and she looks like she visibly pulls in a calming breath before opening the door and finally poking her head through.

"Hi." Her voice comes out squeaky and a little breathless. "Um, this studio is currently closed."

"I'm aware." I arch a brow slightly. "I need to speak with you."

Her eyes widen more if possible. The shade of blue seems extra prominent because of her blue overalls. "Oh. Is everything okay?"

"Can we do this inside?

"Right. Yeah." She visibly blushes and unsurprisingly, it adds to her already endearing personality.

She opens the door wide enough to let me in and I take a look around. There really isn't much. A few paintings are propped up on canvases around the room and the room itself is adorned with flowers and interior decor to make the place more homely. There's another door that leads to what looks like a studio based on what I can see from here. It's small but full of life, kind of like her.

"So." Her voice draws my attention and I turn around to face her again. She's wringing her hands together nervously. They're stained with paint. "What did you need to talk to me about?"

Might as well get this over with so I can get back to my life, a life that has no room for someone like her. "Do you know who I am?"

"Of course. Greg Resnick, the professional boxer."

"I gave you another name the night we met."

"Yes." She clasps her hands behind her back. "Raze."

Hearing her say that sounds wrong. Greg sounds better on her tongue although I have no business having any sort of opinions about this woman.

"That was a mistake. I was careless to give you that information." She says nothing, simply looks at me curiously so I continue. "Be honest—did you try to look into any information about me?"

"I..." Her hesitation tells me everything.

"What did you find? Be honest, Laura."

She jolts a little at the sound of her name, blinking at me like she didn't expect me to remember it. She has no idea I haven't been able to forget her.

"Not a lot." Her voice is like an open book. Every tremble, every hesitant breath, tells me when she's lying. Right now her voice is steady so I know she's speaking the truth. "Honestly, there wasn't anything about you that dated back more than a year. It's like you were a ghost before you started boxing professionally."

"And it's to stay that way," I order firmly. "Did you try searching me up by the name Raze?"

Her cheeks flush. This woman has no poker face whatsoever. I rub a hand tiredly over my forehead.

"Was that wrong?" She whispers. She is so...innocent. Naive.

"Yes." I cross my arms. "And what did you find?"

"Nothing." Her voice wavers. Lie.

"Don't make me ask again."

Her eyes go downcast with guilt. She licks her lips and finally whispers, "One thing. I found one thing."

Her voice is steady. Truth. I nod expectantly. "And?"

"It was an article someone wrote about you. It was in a student journal that talked about crime and violence in the city. They mentioned a Raze that was notorious in the streets and had a reputation for being involved in New York's crime. They made it sound like a legend or something. There was no picture or actual name but since you told me I figured..."

"They were talking about me," I finish for her. I'm not surprised. Nobody knows me by face but I have a lot of influence over this city so the general public know stories, if they know who to listen to at least.

"Is it true?" She lifts her gaze. "What the article said?"

I choose not to answer. "Don't try to find answers about me. I am someone you need to stay away from. You'd only be putting yourself in danger."

With that I stalk past her and head for the door. Only I don't get very far because her warm fingers wrap around my wrist. They're so small they barely meet each other. I stop from the unexpected contact and look over my shoulder in irritation.

"Is Raze who you're battling?" She asks softly. "Is he who you're forced to be?"

I take my hand out of her hold. "I am not forced to be anyone. Enough questions."

"I don't think that's true." She says it like it's a fact. "But...okay."

She clasps her hands behind her back again to obviously let me go. It's what I wanted but I feel...what? Disappointed? I immediately brush it off and go for the door again.

"Oh! I just remembered!"

That might be the loudest I've ever heard her speak. She's usually meek but when I turn around she's on the tips of her toes with excitement. It's new. It also suits her.

"I was really surprised to see you here but only because I was already thinking about you."

My brows just barely inch up in surprise and she visibly stammers when she realizes what her words might have sounded like.

"I mean, not like that. Just...um...come with me? Please?"

What could she possibly want with me? I must look as wary as I feel because she reaches an arm out and gently threads her fingers through mine before pulling me in the direction of the studio I saw earlier. I look down at our joined hands with furrowed brows. Hers are so delicate and colourful and soft. Mine are big and calloused and rough. They look like they don't belong, a representation of the two different worlds we come from. We have no business holding hands.

For some reason that's not enough to make me pull away like I should. Instead I let her guide me to the studio. For such a small person, she tugs my much larger body with a surprising amount of strength. It's kind of amusing.

We enter the studio and it's even smaller than the main room. It's nothing but a shelf full of paints and paintbrushes, a large sheet to cover the floor, and empty canvases stacked to the side. Only one canvas sits in the middle, covered by a cloth, and a stool in front of it that I presume she sits on to paint. She lets go of me and walks to the canvas with a shy expression.

"I'm an artist," She starts. "I'm used to observing people and noticing little details. I see the details in everything. It's kind of how my brain works. Anyway, you were really intense when you approached me the night of your fight and I guess I was mentally stacking up on all your features without meaning to. I got to painting the next day and I finished this morning."

She takes a deep breath like she's nervous. A moment later I understand why.

When she peels the cloth off and reveals the canvas underneath I pause in shock. It's me. She painted me. And there's no mistaking it because it's like looking in a damn mirror. It's nothing more than my face but the painting is entirely accurate. From the crease between my brows, to the way the corner of my lips point down, to my crooked nose that's been broken one too many times, it looks exactly like me. She might as well have taken a photograph.

I glance at her. She's doing it again—chewing the corner of her thumb. Her eyes search mine for a reaction but she will not find one unless I give it. Unlike hers, my poker face is excellent.

"You're very talented," I settle on the obvious. I have no idea what to say. Why would she paint me of all things?

She seems to like the compliment because she grins. It's a breath-taking smile, revealing a little dimple on the top of her cheek. "So you like it?"

"Yes," I answer honestly. I look at the painting again. "Either you've made me more handsome than I am or I had no idea I was a pretty face."

A surprised laugh bubbles out of her. It's a very joyous sound, loud and full of life as she throws her head back. I watch her for a moment observantly. I don't think I have ever laughed like that in my life. She must be a very happy person and that calms me for whatever reason. She seems like she deserves to be happy.

"I don't think you realized you have a sense of humour either." She bites her lip, teeth sinking into her plush mouth. I try not to stare. "Something tells me you're not used to making jokes."

"I'm not."

"Well, you're very good at it. You should consider stand-up comedy if boxing doesn't work out."

"I doubt that would fill the stands like my fighting does."

"I'd be there," She shrugs sweetly.

I eye her curiously. "Not a fan of fights?"

She winces. "That obvious? Not particularly, no."

"Then why were you at mine?"

"My friend dragged me—the one you saw me with? I'm kind of a homebody. I spend everyday cramped up in my studio painting instead of going out and doing things. She wanted me to try something new so it was either going to a boxing match or skinny-dipping."

Her explanation brings forth images I shouldn't be imagining. "And you chose boxing?"

"She wanted to go in the middle of the night," She defends herself. "The water would have been freezing or a shark could have bit my foot off. I figured I was safer in a room full of sweaty men that I'd have to endure an hour with, tops."

I blink. "That...sounds very dramatic."

She laughs sheepishly and taps her temple. "Too much goes on in there."

"I can see that."

"What about you?" She tilts her head. It's as cute as it was the last time she did it. "What do you do for fun?"

Nothing. I can't afford to have fun. I've known my duties since before I could walk and I was trained to fulfill them. I don't say any of it out loud but it's a reminder that I shouldn't be here, putting a woman like her in danger no less. She's too kind for an ill fate and that's all she would get just by being in my presence like this.

"I need to go." I check the time on my watch and straighten out my leather jacket. "Thank you for hearing me out today. And the painting...I'm glad I had the opportunity to see it."

"Oh." She seems disappointed, nibbling her mouth. "You really have to go?"

"Yes." My voice comes out softer than I intended. She wears her heart on her sleeve, this one. She has no reservations, openly showing me that she's enjoying our time and clearly wanting me to stay longer. It thaws me.

Her thumb finds its way to her mouth again. "Do you think...could I maybe see you again?"

My brow creases. "For what?"

A flush takes over her cheeks and nose and she looks down, socked foot messing with the sheet we're standing on. "I don't know. Anything. I paint at the park just down the road sometimes. Maybe you could meet me there. We could eat food and talk."

I blink when realization hits me. She wants to go on a date? With me? I feel a surge of annoyance. Not at her but at myself. If I could be anyone except who I am, I would say yes. Laura is beautiful and kind and I have no doubt men act like idiots to be with her. That she wants to spend time with me hails a very obvious answer—yes. But it's an answer I can't give because she doesn't belong in my world. I couldn't offer her the things she deserves.

"That's not a good idea." They're not words I want to say but I say them. Something odd stirs in my chest at her clear disappointment. "My only business was to make sure you stayed away from me. Seeing you again doesn't help."

Her arms go around her waist almost protectively. She's refusing to meet my eyes. "Oh. Alright. I thought...never mind."

I should walk away. I should. But I'm too curious and maybe a little desperate knowing I won't see her after this. "You thought what?"

"Nothing." She shakes her head.

She looks embarrassed. It bothers me more than it should. I liked it better when she was laughing, brilliant blue eyes twinkling at me. Before I have a chance to think about what I'm doing, I step into her space and catch her chin gently. She sucks in an audible breath when I lift her head up so that she's looking at me.

"Say it," I command softly. "Be honest, Laura."

I might have imagined it but I think her eyes just dropped to my lips. They're back on mine too fast to tell. "I...I thought you might have been interested in me. That's why I asked to see you again. That and...I like you, Greg. I really like what I've seen so far and I want to see more."

Her vulnerability is refreshing. I've never had a woman openly tell me what she thinks about me. I'm not a monk—I fuck when I have the time. I've been with enough women to know what I'm doing. But I only get physical for one purpose and the women I'm with happen to share that purpose. It's get in, get out. Hardly an exchange of words unless they are orders about how I want her to position herself. But that's all women want from me too. Never have I had someone admit they like me. It's so...schoolgirl. But endearing, just like Laura.

"Not in this life, darling." I sweep my thumb across her lip without meaning to and her mouth parts in shock. "We're too different. It would never work. But if this was another world, we would be sharing a very different conversation."

"We could try," She whispers, eyes big and hopeful. She is far too sweet to be at the hands of someone like me.

"We can't." My hand slides to cup her cheek, her skin soft against the roughness of mine.

On a whim I lean down and my lips brush hers. She gasps softly, a sound laced with enough pleasure that I know I can continue, and I add more pressure, kissing her. I'm not sure why I did it but I'm glad because it feels incredible. She feels incredible. She melts into me immediately, warm and inviting and trusting. The way she kisses me back, tentative but excited, makes me forget all the reasons I should stay away. I keep it as appropriate as possible or I know I'll lose control. It's just a gentle caress of my lips on hers but it makes every intimate moment I've had with other women pale in comparison. She's dangerous, this one. I knew she would be.

I pull away too soon. It was a short kiss but one I know I won't be able to forget. Laura's cheeks are flushed, almost glowing with contentment. A little kiss like that was enough to satisfy her. So, so innocent.

"Goodbye, Laura." I keep my eyes on her and raise her hand to my lips, kissing the stains of red and black and grey, the same shades she used to create the painting of me.

"Bye, Greg," She smiles but it looks sad. Unwilling. If I wore my heart on my sleeve like her, I would look the same.

I let her go before I make the mistake of kissing her again. The first one shouldn't have happened either. But I couldn't help myself. One kiss doesn't mean anything anyway and it's all I repeat to myself as I leave her studio, refusing to look back.

Chapter 6

I should not be here. I'm a fucking idiot. I told myself a million times on the drive over to turn around. I told myself I'd stay away and I'm failing miserably.

"Remind me again what this is about?" Mitch yawns beside me, sinking lower against the bench.

I only brought him along because I didn't want to raise suspicions about my whereabouts, especially with my father. He knows everything I do in the day because he demands to stay in the loop, so privacy has never been an option. If anyone, anyone, from the South Bloods found out about this, it would be game over. I have never behaved so recklessly in my life.

"Safety," I answer him.

"Safety," He repeats, less than convinced. He tosses me an exasperated look.

I nod stubbornly. "I just want to make sure she is okay. What if someone saw us talking? She could be in danger because of it."

"So your solution is to stalk her like a creep and increase her chances of getting hurt?"

I punch his arm and he winces because I did not hold back. My glare alone tells him to get his ass back in line. He puts a hand up in surrender, sobering up.

"So, which one is she?"

I look around until I spot her on the far end of the park, sitting on one of the benches. A canvas is propped in front of her as she paints. I follow her line of sight to where a child is sitting in a sandbox and playing by herself. Laura smiles, tilting her head and moving her brush around. I point just barely and Mitch looks in that direction.

"Jesus." He whistles in appreciation. "That picture on the internet did not do her justice. That's a beauty."

My earlier glare returns. I hardly appreciate the way he's talking about her. He must see the murder on my face because he's quick to grab the front of his shirt and put it over his mouth before he says anything else that will earn a punch.

But he's right. She is beautiful. Today she's wearing a red and white polka dot dress held up by two thin straps and ending just above her knee. A loose braid holds her long brown hair away from her face as she paints, though I can already see smidges of colour on the strands. There's some on her face too and once again her hands are entirely covered. She might be passionate about art but she is very messy. It shows she does everything without a care in the world and hardly cares what others think. It's a brave trait and one I wish I had.

I've shown up at this park everyday for the past two weeks but today is the first day I'm seeing her. After she mentioned she paints here, I drove by once a day to catch a glimpse. I told myself what I told Mitch—that I was only concerned about her safety. Though her safety has nothing to do with how I can't seem to forget what it was like to kiss her, or her sweet and inviting personality as she talked to me that day in the studio. She spoke to me like I was anyone else. Not a monster or a killer. Not Raze. I felt like Greg in her presence. A regular man, enamoured by a woman who was far from regular. She has to be the most fascinating person I've ever come across. I shouldn't be as curious as I am about her because it's exactly why I can't seem to stay away.

"What does Abram think we're doing?" Mitch asks quietly. The mention of my father makes my shoulders tighten.

"Patrolling."

"Raze..."

"I know." My jaw ticks, knowing what he will say. He doesn't have to warn me. I know the consequence of what I'm doing. And yet.

Mitch shifts. "What is it about her?"

It's a fair question. I've thought the same to myself for weeks now and I give him the only answer I've been able to come up with. "She is everything I wish I could be."

"And what's that?"

"Kind. Brave. Free."

This is the first time I've admitted to anyone but myself what I truly feel. Never have I made anyone doubt my authority for even a moment. I stiffen when I realize what I've just said but Mitch pats my back.

"Always thought you were too good for this life, brother."

His statement surprises me. "I'm good at what I do. I'm the best leader any gang has seen in years. This is where I belong."

He shrugs. "Maybe not like this. Maybe you were always meant to be a leader but not like this. Not this life."

"I have no choice." My abrupt words are clear that this is the end of our conversation. This will always be my life. I'd be a fool to think otherwise. I'm the son of Abram for fuck's sake. I will always have eyes on my every move. I'm trapped and I've made my peace with it. It is a death wish to question it any further.

"She digs you," Mitch suddenly chuckles. "The way she's looking at you...damn."

I'd been staring at the ground but his words compel me to look where I know Laura is sitting. Immediately my eyes meet hers because she was already looking at me. Mitch is right. The sheer vulnerability on her face allows me to see everything she is feeling. No one has ever looked at me like that.

She smiles shyly and waves a hand, sweet as she is. I didn't mean for her to see me. It's almost time for me to go anyway. I nod back, knowing that I won't be able to resist her now that she knows I'm here.

"We should go," I tell Mitch.

"Wait." He holds a hand out when I try to stand. "She's coming here."

I curse under my breath. "It's a bad idea. Let's go. I need to get back to headquarters."

"I'll cover for you." Mitch fights to hold me in place. "I can come up with something. Just be a guy and hang out with the chick who wants you. For once just do something for yourself, man."

Laura gets closer and I feel a surge of panic. "I can't."

This time Mitch laughs. "You've fought the most dangerous fuckers in this city and you're pissing your pants over a girl half your size. She has you right where she wants you whether we leave or stay. Might as well get something out of it. C'mon."

Fuck. I can feel my reserve slipping. I look at Mitch seriously. "I owe you."

"Like hell. I would've died if you didn't take me under your protection. You saved my life, man. I want you to go live yours now."

I nod my thanks just as Laura stops in front of us. She fidgets with the ends of her braid nervously. "Hey."

I pull my eyes away from her bare legs and look up at her. Fucking hell, she's even prettier up close. I'm out of words already.

"I'm Mitch." The ass-hat veers right in with a charming smile, holding his hand out. "I've heard a lot about you."

I will kill him. He ignores my glare as he shakes hands with Laura. I'm oddly jealous of their contact.

"Oh." Laura sounds surprised. I reluctantly look at her, not sure what to make of the way she's biting the inside of her cheek. "Nice to meet you, Mitch. I'm Laura."

"I know." He winks. Seriously, I will kill him.

"I'm surprised Greg has friends." As soon as the words leave her mouth she covers it with a horrified expression. "Not like that! I just meant, you struck me as a bit of a loner."

"He is," Mitch supplies. "I'm just special. Clearly."

"Clearly," Laura agrees with her dimpled grin. I'm growing increasingly annoyed at how taken Mitch looks with her. It's very unlike me to feel so possessive.

"I'm out." He throws his hands up when he sees the way my nostrils flare. "I can give you an hour, man. No more."

I nod grimly at the reminder. It's more than I expected to have with her so I should be grateful. He tosses one final smile at Laura and jogs off, leaving just us. Laura wastes no time taking his seat beside me.

"Hi," She smiles sweetly. Her eyes graze over me. "You look really handsome."

Why does she always have good things to say about me? I don't deserve them.

"Thank you," I say anyway, not wanting to come across as a dick. "Red suits you."

She looks down at her dress and back up at me, her cheeks now matching her clothes. "Thanks."

I tip my head toward where she was sitting before. "Did you finish your painting?"

"I did," She nods.

"Are you sure you're not wearing half of it?" My lip twitches. It's uncommon for me to be so teasing. It's a foreign feeling but the way Laura giggles makes my discomfort worth it.

"I'm kind of a mess, aren't I?" She scrunches her nose. It reminds me of a rabbit. It's very cute.

"Dirty can be good." My voice sounds deeper than usual and this time I can't look away from her legs. They look long in this dress even though she's so short. My eyes travel back up, over her slender waist and small breasts. Small but perky and all kinds of inviting. By the time I make it back to her face she's wearing that same flushed glow she did when I kissed her. The reminder tugs my gaze to her lips that she's currently nibbling on.

"I thought I wasn't going to see you again," She admits on a whisper.

"Did you want to?" I find myself asking. "See me again?"

"Very much." She fiddles with the ends of her braid some more. "I might have made another painting of you. My friends think I'm obsessed. You must think I'm obsessed. God, why am I still talking?"

Her nervousness is sweet. She ducks her head and I catch her chin, lifting her head back up just like I did when I kissed her. Her blue eyes search mine, wide with anticipation.

"I came to this park everyday hoping to see you," I admit. "I might be obsessed myself, darling."

Her smile disappears behind the hold of her teeth. "You talk so formally. Loosening up would do you some good."

"It was part of my tr—it was how I was raised. Better speaking etiquette commands authority. Respect."

"You already have my respect," She murmurs. "Loosen up."

"How?"

She squints one eye. "It gives me butterflies when you call me darling. But it also sounds like something a grandfather would say. Maybe lose the g?"

My brows crease. "Darlin'?"

Her eyes light up. "That's it. That was so you."

"I don't think so. That sounded awful. Besides, I'm not southern."

"Oh, come on. It might grow on you. Try it again?"

This is beyond uncomfortable. But the hopeful way Laura looks at me, the way she gradually scoots closer to me, is all the convincing I need. "Okay, darlin'."

She grins and I'm greeted with that dimple of hers. "God, that was perfect. You don't think so?"

I think you're perfect, I want to say. Instead I shake my head and look away. I'm losing my head over this girl and fast. She might be the most dangerous thing I've ever done in my life.

She crosses one leg over the other, her foot entangling around mine. Her flip-flops show off her red toenails and even her feet have smidges of paint. I hold back a smile.

"Can I ask you something?" She asks softly. I turn my head to look at her. Her face is closer than it was before and all I can think about is kissing her again.

"Yes," I say, trying to stay on track.

"What made you come back? You sounded like you really wanted me to stay away. I listened to you—I didn't search you up again or anything."

"The truth is I should still be staying away. My being here is a very bad idea."

"Then how come you're here?"

I search her face, so open as she waits for my answer. Her honesty makes me want to give it back. "It seems you've made quite an impression on me. Enough that I won't take my own advice."

"Oh." She looks away but I catch her hint of a smile. "I'm sorry."

"I'm not."

She looks at me again, taking in a deep breath. "Can I ask you another question?"

That she asks to ask a question every time is very amusing. It's no wonder I'm constantly fighting smiles. "Yes."

"Why did you kiss me that day?"

"Because I wanted to," I say without missing a beat. Maybe I am starting to loosen up around her. I can't seem to think straight. "I thought I wouldn't be seeing you again."

"And now that you're back...do you regret it?"

"No," I shake my head, holding her eyes. "Nothing could have stopped me from kissing you."

I think my answer appeases her. She presses her lips to stop a smile but that dimple still makes an appearance. She whispers, "One more question?"

"Yes, Laura?"

"Do you want to kiss me right now? Because I really want to kiss y—"

I cut her off by grabbing the back of her head and crushing my lips to hers. This time she's not surprised. She smiles against my mouth and kisses me back, small hands cupping my face as she wiggles closer. I wrap an arm around her waist and lift her weight effortlessly, setting her onto my lap. She sighs in contentment, arms going around my neck, and I take the kiss deeper in a way I didn't allow myself to last time. I part her lips with my tongue and she gives me entry, opening her mouth. My tongue meets hers and I feel like I'm on fire from the inside out when she moans quietly but sweetly. My grip on her waist tightens. I want nothing more than to rub her hips into mine but then she'd feel the evidence of my arousal and I don't want to scare her away. We're also in public.

Shit. We're in public.

I pull away quickly, breathing hard. Laura is panting too and she looks at me in concern. "Are you okay?"

The reminder that I can't be with her in the open is one I don't welcome. For a moment I forgot what a danger I am to her, how selfish I'm being.

"You're not safe with me," I tell her truthfully. She deserves it. "This is just as bad of an idea as it was two weeks ago. I don't know what I'm thinking."

"You don't feel dangerous to me," She whispers, index finger dragging across my lips. "What are you running from? Maybe I can help."

She's far too good for me. Far too sweet. And I'll never be good enough for her.

"We shouldn't do this." I catch her hand, kissing her knuckles. They're brown and yellow today.

Her eyes have become saddened. She tilts her head at me, fingers playing with the scruff on my face. She's very touchy. Affectionate.

"Mitch said he can give you an hour, right? Will you spend that hour with me?"

My chest expands with a rough intake of air. "That would be asking too much from you."

"Not if that's what I want to give you. Please, Greg?"

I hesitate, thumbs absentmindedly stroking her hipbones. I want to say no. It's on the tip of my tongue to say no. But this is my chance, isn't it? Mitch is covering for me and Laura is here right now. If I don't use this time I may not get it again. It will only be torture getting a tease of her when I can't have her completely but it's better than nothing.

"One hour," I relent. "And no place too public."

The grin she gives me is overwhelming. She's so radiant and I'm compelled to smile back but I manage to keep a straight face. "Deal."

We end up back at her studio. It's the only place we could think of where we would be hidden away. Laura flips the sign on the front door back to closed and brings the blinds down. I appreciate how serious she is about the privacy I asked for. There was no hesitation on her end, no questions. How can someone as good as her even exist?

"Have I ruined your plans for today?" I ask.

"I normally don't have any." Her laughter is partly self-conscious. "You haven't ruined anything."

How ironic her words are. If she only knew who I really was, she wouldn't be anywhere near me right now.

"What's wrong?" She looks at me worriedly. I know my face is passive right now despite what's going on in my head. Already she's getting far too good at reading me.

"Nothing." I brush it off. I might be taking all kinds of risks here but the less Laura knows about my life, the better. Withholding the truth is for her own good. "I admit, I'm curious about the painting you mentioned."

There's that rosy blush again. "You want to see it?"

"I'd like to, yes."

She nods, clasping my fingers between hers again. She doesn't think twice about touching me. She does it with complete ease and trust. Selfishly, I bask in it. I really am a bastard.

We get to her studio room and, like last time, there's a canvas propped in the middle. Not covered so I immediately see the painting and my brows go up in surprise. This one is even better than the last. It's a full portrait—me standing in the ring and fists raised at the ready. Black paint surrounds the image of me and makes me the clear focus of the painting. It's intense and powerful.

"Christ," I mutter. "You really are incredible."

I can feel the rapid flutter of her pulse where our wrists touch, hands still joined. "You think so?"

I nod, reluctantly letting go of her hand. Only because I might yank her against me and kiss the hell out of her otherwise. I need to cool down a little. I get closer to the painting, impressed with the accuracy of the details. My face is sketched to perfection and the contours of my body as well. I lift my shirt up to my neck with one hand, looking back and forth in comparison.

"Looks the same," I comment and glance over at her.

She's chewing the edge of her thumb again, eyes trained on my revealed skin. There's heat in them and a lot of appreciation. A small noise comes out of me, like a chuckle but not quite, and Laura blushes before quickly looking away.

"Stop." I take hold of her thumb and draw it away from her mouth.

"Sorry," She apologizes, breathless. "Bad habit. I do that when I'm nervous."

"Am I making you nervous?"

"No. I mean, kind of."

"How's that?" I ask in all seriousness.

She gestures to my body. "You know...you're so...wow. I'm tempted to drop and do twenty to get at your level."

The corner of my mouth twitches. I take a step closer to her, hand curving around the bend in her waist and tugging her against me. She sucks in a breath but doesn't take her eyes away from mine.

"You are beautiful," I assure her. I don't understand why she would ever think otherwise. "I'm the one that might be in over my head here."

"Doubtful," She whispers, smiling shyly.

I shake my head, dropping my voice several octaves. "I mean it, Laura. If I had it my way, I would rip this dress off your body right here. Maybe take you against that wall. I'm the furthest thing from the respectable gentleman you deserve."

Her breath catches, eyes widening innocently. There's no mistaking the desire in them, however.

"Maybe I don't want a respectable gentleman," She murmurs tentatively.

My eyes fall shut. I feel like I'm in pain. "Don't tempt me."

I feel her hands glide up my chest before cupping the back of my neck. Her fingers play with the tuft of my hair, eliciting a groan from me. The barest touch and I'm at her mercy. Women have done far more and rarely accomplished this kind of reaction from me. It only confirms that Laura is unlike anyone I've ever met.

When I feel her body swaying I open my eyes, confused. "What are you doing?"

"Dancing," She grins.

Though my body is completely still, she's not undeterred. "There is no music."

"Who says you need music to dance? I make my own rules." She juts her chin out in an attempt to look tough. It's getting harder to conceal my smiles around her. "I'm a rebel like that."

"Very scary," I confirm seriously and she throws her head back in laughter. I watch her for a moment, compelled. Hypnotized. "I don't dance, you know."

"That's okay." And I know she means it too. "Want to play some poker instead?"

This time I can't contain the way my features shift. My eyebrows jump up in obvious surprise. "You play?"

"Who doesn't?"

"Well, you never struck me as the type."

"I'm actually really good. Just saying."

I shake my head slowly. "I've been playing since I was ten. You don't want to play with me unless you are willing to lose."

She raises a brow a little saucily, challenge clear in her eyes. "Let's see what you got, Raze."

She beats me three times in a row, clearing my pockets and all the cash I have on me. What a fucking woman.

Chapter 7

That one hour eventually turned into one month as time went by. The moment I found myself able to spare some time, I would go to Laura. Every time I told her the same thing—it would be the last time I'd see her. And every time I'd find show up again, either at her studio or that park. I might have felt like an idiot if she didn't light up with relief and excitement whenever I returned.

Typically I see her once or twice a week. Never more than an hour because that alone is more than I can spare. Most of the time we stay in her studio. It's small and quaint and hidden in this bustling city. A couple of times she was able to convince me to go out, whether to sit in a park somewhere or try disgusting street foot that she insists I need to be a true New Yorker. Sometimes we are simply in each other's company. She will paint if she's inspired and I will train—if I can keep my eyes off her long enough to. Though I've caught her eyeing my body on more than one occasion, thumb ever present in the space between her teeth, so my own ogling is not out of place.

I steal touches when I can. Kiss her senseless every time I have to leave. Never more or I'd lose all control. I refuse to get intimate with her based on lies. She doesn't deserve that. She deserves the truth but I am a coward and I haven't been able to give it to her. I'm sure on some level she suspects something, but she has no idea how deep my demons run. If I was a good man I would not let her get caught in them. But this past month I've learned I'm very selfish when it comes to her.

I'm also falling for her, hard. Her goodness is addicting. After being surrounded by nothing but blood and death and vengeance my entire life, she is like a breath of fresh air for my charred lungs. I can't stop coming back. What's worse is she lets me when she shouldn't.

I am not sure what she sees in me. I don't bring anything worthwhile to the proverbial table. I live a dangerous lifestyle, surrounded by dangerous men, son of the most dangerous man in New York. I am not worth all this trouble but she has never made me feel that way. She has this way of making me feel better than I truly am. Sometimes I wonder if I am capable of being the man she believes I can be. It's not a promising thought but I entertain it often. Too often, especially when it should not cross my mind at all. But I forget about all of that when it's just us.

"Stay still," She grumbles now. She's become less shy with me and I've learned she has a tendency to be bossy. I honestly enjoy it because I usually do the bossing. It's a nice change of pace.

"I am still," I counter even as I shift for the hundredth time. I can't help it. I've been sitting like this for nearly an hour. It also doesn't help that Laura is bent forward as she paints and I have a clear view of her cleavage. It is a miracle in itself that we haven't done anything except kiss. I always feel animalistic around her but manage to refrain myself.

She sighs and straightens up, shaking her head at me. A normal person would be annoyed but Laura has unbelievable patience. She's too gentle to ever get upset with me, which is why I walk on eggshells around her for fear that I'll hurt her somehow. If I did I would never forgive myself.

"I'll stop torturing you," She teases. "I can do the rest from memory."

I push up off the ground and get to my feet, walking to her. "Really? You must think about me often."

"Way too often," She agrees with a grin. She is also unapologetically honest which I appreciate more than she knows. I'm surrounded by liars, myself included.

I push my fingers through her hair and away from her face, raising a brow. "You're covered in paint again, darlin'."

She barely manages to suppress a smile at the term of endearment. Unsurprisingly she was right. I did get used to it and it doesn't sound so bad anymore.

"I'll go wash myself." She hops off the stool and brushes past me with a wink. I watch as her dress swishes around her. Today it's white with puffy short sleeves and the hem is higher than her other dresses. My eyes have been glued to her legs all day. I think she knows how infatuated I am with her legs and is trying to torture me. If so, mission fucking accomplished.

I feel my brows pull in when she opens the door to her studio and dashes outside. A crazy thunderstorm is happening which is why we're staying inside today. What the hell is she doing?

I jog to the front door, opening it but staying inside. I watch incredulously as she holds her arms out beside her and spins around in circles, her airy laugh travelling to me. She's already soaked to the bone.

"Laura!" I raise my voice above the thunder. "Get back inside!"

"Join me outside!" She calls back, waving a hand to gesture at me. "It's just rain, tough guy!"

Crazy woman. "You're going to get sick. Come here."

Her head shakes in defiance, teeth sinking into her bottom lip. She pushes her hands into her hair and lets her head fall back, eyes closed and face tipped to the sky as rain pours down on her.

My mouth runs dry at the sight of her. She looks ethereal. At some point she kicked off her shoes so her feet are bare and I can see the white polish on her toes that matches her dress. A dress that's currently drenched and completely see-through. My breath knocks out of me when I notice her white lacy underwear and bra and how they mold so perfectly to her soft curves. Fuck, what I wouldn't give to strip her bare and worship every inch of her. It's suddenly hard to breathe, to think.

She brings her head back down, lips parting when she catches the look on my face. Even from here I can see the way her chest is slightly heaving. Thick and wet locks stick to her face and her eyes burn bluer than I've ever seen them. They're full of want, for me.

Fuck the rain. I stalk up to her with quick and long strides, barely registering the ice cold water that pelts down on me. I welcome it and the way it cools down my body that's running hotter than it usually does. I feel like I'm on fire, my impatient steps closing the distance between us. I bend low and grab the back of her thighs, hoisting her up and earning her surprised gasp as she wraps her legs around me. A second later I take that sweet sound all for myself when I slam my mouth against hers.

I fucking devour her mouth, the kiss a messy clash of teeth and lips. Laura kisses me back just as hungrily and her fingers grip onto my hair to bring my face as close as possible to hers. Our lips slip and slide against each other, wet as they are from the rain. I briefly register the crash of thunder above us but I don't care. Not when I have her in my arms like this. Not when I feel her body pressing into mine, her softness nestling into my hard ridges like we were made for each other. I can't get enough and my tongue battles hers desperately. Her answering sigh is all I need to keep going.

I turn us around, pressing her body into the wall behind her to hold her up. My hand grips the back of her head to angle it better, tip her face further back so I can get deeper into her mouth. Her hands clutch the front of my soaked shirt and even through the cloth I can feel the heat of her touch. Another clap of thunder rings out but it's nothing compared to the storm inside of me. The electricity between our every touch fiercely rivals the strikes of lightning around us. I have never felt anything like this.

I only wrench my mouth away because the kiss is so intense, so full, that I feel like I have no air left. Laura and I both pull in harsh gasps when we separate, panting hard as we stare at each other. She is so beautiful, it hurts. I never want to stop looking at her.

But the rest of her body is just as tempting and I cannot resist. My head dips low to capture the skin of her neck between my lips and I suck feverishly, the taste of salty rain sitting heavy on my tongue. It's mixed with a twinge of vanilla, the taste of her, and I suck harder. Greedily. Like my life depends on it, and I think it does. Her moan is sweet and so responsive that I feel how much it hardens me. My hips rock forward slowly, just to test the waters, and Laura gasps. Her thighs grip my body in place like she never wants to let go. Neither do I.

"Greg," She sighs breathily. Her arms go around my neck and her cheek presses against mine. It's only then that I feel her body shaking slightly. Goosebumps dot her arms but she doesn't complain. Just holds me tighter.

"Time to go inside," I murmur. I pull back to look at her, my thumb playing with her bottom lip that is now swollen and reddened thanks to me. "You're soaked."

"More than you know," She whispers shyly, head ducking. I curse in misery and yank her head back up to kiss her again. She is so unbelievably sexy without even trying. There is so much I wish to do to her. Dirty, unspeakable things. I would ravish her so completely if given the chance.

I pull away at another round of thunder, this one the loudest yet. I push away my drenched hair from my forehead and meet her eyes. "You really will get sick. Is there anywhere I can take you for a change of clothes?"

"Home," She answers without hesitation. Her thumbs sweep across my cheekbones and she swallows hard. "Take me home."

Laura's apartment is very small. Just a simple one bedroom with an open kitchen. She's down the hall now and I can hear the shower running. I'm seated at the dining table, my leg bouncing with nerves as I look through my messages. I have been gone for two hours now and that does not bode well. I have lots of business I need to return to and everyone is looking for me. I only respond to Mitch, seeing as he is the only one who knows where I am.

Mitch: Next shipment arrives in an hour. You need to get back.

Me: Thirty minutes at most. I'll make it.

Mitch: You missed the meeting too. Told your father you were caught in a brawl so look banged up. He already doesn't believe me.

Fuck. The meeting. The one I was supposed to run. How in the hell did I forget? The lines are blurring too fast and I'm forgetting my responsibilities.

"Fuck." I let my phone clatter on the table, not bothering with a response. I scrub my hands over my face roughly. I don't know what to do anymore. If Father ever discovers my distractions are because of a girl, he would go as far as to kill her without hesitation. Nothing stands in the way of Abram Resnick. His son going soft will ruin the credibility of this family, the credibility of our reputation and the South Bloods, and he would never let that happen. He has far too many enemies and the only reason he is still alive is because he is feared. If that gets taken away, he shouldn't expect to live very long. He'd stop at nothing to prevent that.

"Is everything okay?"

I look up at the sound of Laura's voice. She walks over to me and I drink in the sight of her. She's in a simple t-shirt and pair of pyjama shorts, face fresh and without makeup, and the most beautiful woman I've ever laid eyes on. Yes, I'm going soft for her. Yes, she makes me reckless. But any man would lose his mind for her so who can blame me?

"I have to go," I tell her when she stops in front of me. I reach up to slide my hands to the backs of her thighs, her skin like velvet under my touch. Laura's breath audibly catches.

"Really?" She asks with clear disappointment. She searches my face. "Is it your father?"

She does not know much aside from the fact that he controls my life and I don't want her anywhere near him. I think she understands on some level that he is a dangerous man.

"Among other things," I answer vaguely. "I have..."

"Business," She finishes for me. It's the response I always give her so she's familiar with it now.

"Yes. Business. You'll be okay?"

"Of course. Thank you for driving me."

I nod, looking around at her apartment again. It's so quiet. "I recognize it's unfair to ask this when I share nothing about myself but where's your family?"

She doesn't seem offended that I asked. Instead she sits sideways on my lap, leaning into me. I wrap an around her and absentmindedly play with the ends of her hair while I wait for her to answer.

"I was left on the steps of an orphanage when I was a few months old," She starts, surprising me. "Up until I was eighteen I went through a lot of foster families. The constant change and never sticking in one place really took a toll on my self-confidence so I acted out a lot. I used to be caught up in some messy crowds. I had a mean alcohol tolerance once upon a time. A record full of vandalizing and B&E's so no one wanted the troubled girl."

My brows are pushed as high as they can go. Laura notices and laughs. Again, not offended.

"I know. I was a far cry from who I am now. Even I can't believe it sometimes."

"What changed?"

She chews the edge of her thumb but I don't bother stopping her. "When I was old enough to leave the foster system, I was given information on who my birth parents were. My father was some hotshot businessman who accidentally knocked up my mother, who was a hooker mind you. He couldn't deal with the embarrassment so he paid her off to stay away. Signed a non-disclosure and everything. My mother tried raising me but I guess she just wasn't cut out for it so she gave me up. That was that."

Bastards. The unfairness of it angers me and my fists clench on their own accord. "Where are they now?"

"I was too scared to try and contact them initially. I mean, neither of them wanted me, you know? Plus I was a mess. So I kept my head down and got through college, hoping to graduate and maybe impress them. My father was easier to track down because he was a big name. He looked ready to drop dead when he found out who I was. An illegitimate child would have been the scandal to take him down so he did what he does best—threw some money at me to stay quiet. I remember that day so vividly, Greg. I felt like throwing up when I realized he would never want me."

"Shit." I pull her closer when her voice catches, pressing my lips to her temple. I hear a small sniffle and my chest fucking cracks opens. "I'm so sorry, baby."

"That's okay," She whispers and rubs my arm. Comforting me even when she's the one who's falling apart. How did she get to be so selfless after the life she's had? Her bravery is something I could never hope to achieve.

"I didn't want to take the money. It would be a reminder that it was my replacement for a father. I tried tracking down my mother next, hoping to soothe the pain of rejection but then I found out she had passed away already. Some kind of illness. I think breast cancer? So the money became the only thing I could get out of all of that and I took it. I couldn't deny needing it, especially since I had crazy student loans."

But she would have chosen having parents any day and we both know it. I stay quiet as she starts to draw circles on my chest. Her hands are pale and completely free of paint smudges. It looks wrong and so unlike her.

"After that I did a lot of soul searching," She admits. "I know I never knew my mother but her death shook me. All I could think was that she died without knowing me and how I turned out. I took whatever was left of my birth father's money and travelled. Cheap flights and a lot of backpacking became my only friends for the next couple years. I just...lived. I didn't want to end up like my mother—I didn't want to die while missing such big parts of me. I wanted to live a life I was proud of and be a person I was proud of. I straightened myself out with a lot of discipline and learned to appreciate the simplicity of life. I'm not who I was but...everybody has a past, Greg. And it doesn't make us bad people."

She sits up and looks at me, cupping my face. I struggle to meet her eyes because I know she's talking about me now. I feel like she can see right through me.

"I'd never judge you. You know that, right? I can't promise I won't see you differently but that's not a bad thing. It just means I'll know who you truly are and that's all I really want. I want to know the man I'm falling in love with."

Fuck me. My breath knocks out of me so suddenly that I almost can't catch it again. I stare at her, completely dumbfounded. "What?"

"I also don't want to live a life of regrets," She continues, ignoring the way she just knocked me on my ass. "So I say whatever's on my mind. I just want to be honest with you. I'm sorry if it seems like I'm coming on too strong."

I pride myself in being good with words. Knowing what to say and how to say it is a huge factor in being a leader. I need the ability to negotiate, make deals, talk people off, convince others. But right now it is as if my vocabulary doesn't exist. The words are tumbling around my head but I can't reach them. I can't speak.

"Go," Laura whispers. I think she realizes I'm not going to give a response anytime soon. But I think she also knows what I'm feeling right now because she searches my eyes with a small, amused smile. "I don't want you to get caught in more trouble."

I nod reluctantly and she stands, fingers threading through mine. It's a silent trip to the elevator and once we're in it, she does nothing but lean back against me. I feel like I should say something but she isn't demanding anything so that takes the pressure off. She walks me out the lobby and to the front where my car is parked. I hesitate but she gives me a little shove, laughing.

Once I'm in my car, she leans downs and rests her arms on the open window. "Is this the part where you say we can't see each other again?"

Though her tone is teasing, nothing about this is funny anymore. Nor is it a game. This is real and it has been a long time since I've had something real.

"No." My gruff response surprises her. "I won't kid myself anymore. I'll come back, Laura. Every time I leave."

She blinks a couple of times before her lips take on a shy smile. Her eyes drop and she nods. "Okay."

I start my car and she backs up, arms crossed and watching me. As I drive off I meet her eyes one more time and she blows me a kiss. My smile is immediate because even though I'm dreading going back to headquarters and facing my father, the thought of her will make it so much fucking easier.

Chapter 8

"Stop!" Father barks at me.

My shoulders tighten at the menace in his voice and I stop my hand from going any further, letting it drop instead of opening the door. Impatience like I've never known it knocks into me and I allow my jaw to tick before clearing my face of any emotion, turning around to face him. His face is reddened with anger and he jabs a finger toward his office, a silent command to follow him.

I glare daggers into the back of his head while he leads us. As the days go by I despise him more and more. I despise my life and everything about it. I'm caught in the hold of the shackles he's placed on me since birth. He has always made me believe that this is where I belong. It wasn't until Laura that I truly questioned it and now that I have, the answer has never been more clear—I do not want this life anymore. I don't want anything to do with my father or his way of life. I've always forgiven his wrongdoings, looked the other way even when I knew he was a dangerous and vile man, but it's becoming harder to ignore and I can't keep doing it.

What makes a man this way? What makes a man feel powerful in the presence of the fallen? It's cowardice at best yet my father believes he is strong. What's worse is he has all of New York believing it, myself included.

Deception is a funny thing. It makes you believe that lies are truth and truths are lies. That's why the world looks new when you realize you have been fooled the whole time. And I have been such a fool.

I close the door behind me while Father takes a seat at his desk. He's practically foaming at the mouth, eyes narrowed on me when I make my way to stand in front of him. That look—as humiliating as it is to admit to myself—used to terrify me. I've always thought of my father as untouchable. Now? Not so much. Not at all, even. I merely blink at him, not the least bit undeterred. He notices, if the flash in his eyes is any indication.

"What do you want?" I break the silence with my words. They're spoken casually, lacking the usual respect I give him.

Father's face contorts. "You will watch the way you speak to me, boy. It is not wise to get on my bad side."

As if any goodness exists in him. "I have somewhere to be."

"Don't you always?" He mocks. "I've been watching you. You disappear for hours at a time, neglecting your duties as leader. There is nothing more important than your loyalty to the South Bloods. Nothing. Yet you've made this family a second priority and I will not stand for it. Come clean while I have the patience to be lenient with you."

Or what, I want to say. I bite the side of my tongue to stop myself.

"My duties as leader will always be your business. But what I do on my own time is not your concern."

"Enough! Now, you listen—"

"You listen!" I smack my hands on the surface of his desk and he just barely jolts in surprise. "You are a suffocating man. You are unbelievably selfish. This is exactly why Mother drowned herself in a fucking bathtub to escape the nightmare that you are. I will not suffer the same fate! I complete the duties required of me but that is all you get. No more."

His eyes narrow on me, jaw ticking at the mention of Mother. It is the first I've spoken of her in the ten years since her death. I can see his anger increasing tenfold.

"Are you planning to betray us?" He inquires. "Working with another gang perhaps? Don't think I won't find out. Don't think I'll stop at anything to figure out."

"You do that." I straighten up, raising a brow. "However, I do wonder what the others might think if they found out Abram doesn't have control over his own son. What would they think of you or your leadership? Do what you must. Send our men to follow me. Have them wire my clothing. But at what cost?"

His fists clench, eyes blazing. I've never seen him so out of sorts. I lean forward and jab a finger roughly to his temple.

"Everything that's in there, I know. You trained me, remember? I will always be ten steps ahead of you. I will always know what actions you will take before you've so much as thought of them. Don't ever threaten me again."

I don't give him a chance to answer. Without sparing another glance I turn on my heel and stalk out of his study, slamming the door behind me. My chest expands as I pull in a deep breath. That was probably the first time I've ever stood up for myself. I feel weak in the knees.

"Raze." I recognize the deep voice and turn around, not surprised to find Byron walking towards me.

"I take it you heard that." It's not a question.

Byron rubs a hand down his jaw. "Think about what you're doing here. I've been sensing for some time now that you have no interest being our leader anymore. You have to understand why I don't agree."

"Your choices are yours just as mine are mine."

"I understand. The South Bloods have thrived off your leadership but son...old blood will always win. No matter what you do, everyone will follow the command of your father before yours. Including me."

It's nothing I don't already know, though I can't deny the unsettling feeling it gives me. "It's not like I'm leaving."

His expression tells me he doesn't believe me. Instead he crosses his arms and levels me with a serious look, voice low. "Is it a girl?"

Protectiveness like I've never known it knocks into me. I don't want these fuckers anywhere near Laura. I don't want them to even think about her. "No."

"You look ready to slice me open," He sighs deeply and pinches the bridge of his nose. "You have been very good to me. Never undermined me and let me take command when you saw it fit. For that reason, I will keep the rest of our men away from you. But figure out what you're going to do and fast. In this life, everything is life or death. You hesitate one second too long and you can guess which side you'll end up on."

"I know." I swallow hard.

"We are loyal to our men but we are a dangerous breed. Some of these men are bloodthirsty, lacking a soul. You know we kill for sport so don't give us a reason to go after you. Tread carefully, son. I won't enjoy having to bury you if you don't."

I nod, not sure what to say. The truth is I'm acting on adrenaline alone. I don't know what I want. Not yet. All I know is that there's a beautiful girl I don't know how to leave behind, and dragging her down with me is not an option. I've been trapped all my life, but this is a bind I truly don't know how to escape.

"What are we doing?" Laura asks quizzically.

I close the door of the gym I rented out behind me, peering out to make sure no one familiar is nearby. Though I doubt I have to worry because I trust Byron's word that he'll help me keep my trail cold. Doesn't hurt to check.

"How much do you know about self-defence?" I ask her.

"Does my pepper spray count?"

"It's a start," I chuckle. I come to a stop in front of her and cross my arms. "I am going to show you basic fighting moves. All within your capabilities."

"How come?"

"It's a very good skill to have. Besides, I would feel a lot better knowing you have some sort of understanding of how to defend yourself."

She's quiet for a moment. "Your lifestyle is that dangerous?"

"Yes," I say solemnly, not surprised that she caught on to why we're doing this. "I would never let anything happen to you. Never. But I also think if fighting is something you can learn, then you should. Teaching will always hold more value than having something done for you."

She tilts her head. "Catch a fish for a man, you feed him for a day. Teach a man how to fish, you feed him for a lifetime."

My lips tug up with a surge of pride and I tuck her hair behind her ear. "Exactly, darlin'."

"Okay." She blows out a breath, anxiously running her hands down her workout clothes I made her change into. "Just don't laugh at me if I suck."

"No promises."

"Jerk." She shoves me with a laugh. "What first?"

"Fighting stance. The way you distribute your weight will make all the difference in how your moves are carried out. If you do it right, it will come to you easy and naturally."

For the next half an hour I do nothing but teach her how to get into position. Legs apart, hips lined, shoulders loose. I have her switch from all kinds of positions back into stance. Casually walking—stance. Sitting down—stance. Backed into a corner—stance. She's tense in the beginning but gradually loosens herself until it comes to her instinctively. And she does it damn well.

"Good," I nod in approval when she has it down. "Now get back into stance and I'll show you how to carry out three basic and effective moves."

"There's more?" She groans. My lips twitch.

"We hardly did anything."

"To you! I sit it one spot and paint. This is the most movement I've had in who knows how long."

I shake my head. "Then let's make a deal. After this, we will do an activity of your choosing. Anything."

Her brows go up. "Really? Anything?"

"I give you my word."

She taps her chin, eyeing me with an expression I can't read. "That's a very convincing argument. You negotiate well."

I shrug. "As a leader, I have to."

She blinks then and I realize this is one of the first pieces of information I've offered about myself and what I really do. I wait for the regret to come but it doesn't. More like relief, if I am being honest.

"I bet you make a great leader," She whispers. "I can see that in you."

I find it amusing that I've never truly wanted to lead the South Bloods yet with Laura's compliment I feel pride. She makes me feel greater than I am.

"Thank you." I clear my throat. "Do we have a deal?"

"Deal." She points a finger at me. "Anything."

"I don't even want to know what's going through your head right now," I mutter and she laughs. Something tells me I should be wary.

The deal was a good idea because she sobers up and listens to my instructions dutifully. I show her the most basic defence moves that she can perform with ease and would be the most efficient if she needs to make a getaway.

First I teach her how to free herself if grabbed from behind. Head-butt with the back of the head to the nose, turn and throat-punch, kick to the balls and run. Then I teach her how to get away if she's grabbed by one arm and only has use of the other. Poke out both eyes of the offender with fingers, then heel-palm strike to the nose upwards to send the attacker back. Finally, I teach her the elbow strike for when the attacker is too close and she has limited use of her arms and legs. One simple strike of the elbow to the jaw, chin, or temple is effective enough to push the attacker back.

It takes a lot of practice because Laura has to put in more force than she anticipated and she has to really make use of her core strength but it's a good first lesson. A couple of more and she'll be a pro.

"Excellent." I crouch down where Laura is splayed on the floor, panting hard. I smooth the strands of hair stuck to her forehead away from her face. "You did very well."

"I hate you," She groans. "I am so going to feel this first thing in the morning."

"It's a rewarding type of pain."

"Speak for yourself, buddy. Not all of us are fighters."

"You are," I say softly. "More than you know."

A small smile appears on her mouth as she eyes me. "I could say the same to you."

The comment is a reminder of earlier today. I sit down on the floor, leaning back on my palms. I know I should be more mindful in the information I indulge her in but I can't deny wanting to share what happened. I don't know when it happened but Laura has quickly become the person I want to share everything with.

"I stood up to my father today," I tell the ground more so than her. I can feel her eyes on me. "I haven't done that in...well, ever. And you want to know something, darlin'? He didn't scare me one fucking bit. I knew I had the upper hand. I knew in that moment he has always made me feel weaker than I am. I think he has always known that I could outdo him if I recognized my abilities, so he made sure I never did. He's not as untouchable as he thinks. I won't allow him to control me anymore."

Laura sits up, resting her chin on her knees. "How do you feel? Now that you've stood up to him."

"Like I should have done it a long time ago," I answer truthfully. We're quiet for a few moments, both of us lost in our own thoughts. "Do you ever feel like you don't belong? Even if you know it is your place, your family, you just don't fucking fit?"

"All the time." She smiles sadly. "It's how I felt about every foster family I was thrown in. Not all of them were bad. The family I lived with for the last two years I was in the system were really great. We send each other cards on holidays even now. I have nothing against them but...I always felt like an intruder. I knew I could earn my place with them if I just accepted it but it never felt right. It was like forcing together two puzzle pieces that looked like they could work, but you knew never would."

"Exactly." It's like she put every thought in my head into a tangible sentence that suddenly makes sense. I know Laura does not know much about my life but she's still managed to understand me far better than anyone else I've ever known. "How did you stop feeling that way?"

She thinks about it for a moment. "Finding myself. When you've spent your entire life being defined by others, you don't know who you really are. I had to get away and leave everything behind."

"Did it work?"

"I think so," She shrugs a little self-consciously. "I think I've come a long way from who I used to be. I think this is who I've always been."

I nod, a little envious of her surety in this moment. My voice is somber when I admit, "I don't know who I am."

"I do." She moves to sit on my lap, cupping my face and forcing me to meet her gaze. "You're a leader. A teacher. You are a good man, Greg. I think you were always meant to help others in some way. But you can only do that if you help yourself first."

I draw in a breath, setting my forehead to her collarbone and breathing her in. She gives me the peace I crave. "And if I don't know how?"

"Then let me help you," She whispers. Her arms go around my neck and she holds me to her. I don't think I've ever been held. "Let me help you the way you've helped me."

She has no idea that is what she's been doing this whole time.

Chapter 9

"It seems it's my turn to wonder what we're doing."

Laura casts me a nervous smile but continues to tug me forward, offering no elaboration.

I was definitely a little skeptical when she asked to meet me later than we usually do. It's well past midnight and, though I had to pull a few strings to slip away, I managed. Now we are at a beach of all places. I think the rebel still exists in Laura because she snuck us in like a pro and I have to admit, I was impressed. And turned on, admittedly.

She stops close to the shore and takes my shoulder bag from me, dropping it on the sand. It has a change of clothes that she asked I bring and I suddenly put two and two together.

"Are we going for a swim?"

"Of sorts." She looks down, her flip-flops digging into the sand. "Remember when I first met you and explained I was only at your match because I didn't want to go with another option?"

"Skinny-dipping." I bite the inside of my cheek. Apparently I underestimated how much of her rebellious side still exists. "I'm surprised."

"But willing?" She offers a little grin, gesturing to the water. "I'm still too chicken but I thought it would be fun if we did it together. Another memory."

"Piling up on those?" I ask softly. My hands slide to cup her cheeks and gently tilt her face up. The look in her eyes is a little shy and a lot endearing.

"Yeah," She whispers. She links her fingers through mine. "Help me make another?"

I nod and lean down to capture her lips, pulling her closer when her arms go around my neck. I can't believe it's already been three months since I met her, since she showed up at my boxing match and spun me on my ass with a simple smile. She's not the only one collecting memories.

I reluctantly let her go when she pushes her palms against my chest and takes a couple of steps back. She faces the water and starts stripping, pulling off her short flowery dress in one smooth motion. My breath stalls in my lungs at the sight of her in just an underwear and bra. Her body is beautiful, so inviting, that I have to shove my hands in my pockets to stop myself from grabbing her. Laura notices me watching and even in the dark, I can see the way her cheeks darken in colour.

"Stop staring." She turns away and I chuckle under my breath, holding my hands up in surrender.

I give her my back and waste no time stripping. I'm a lot less shy than her so I don't really mind as I get rid of my shirt and jeans, kicking off my boxers without a second thought. It's late summer so the breeze is chilly but not unbearable. I glance over my shoulder at Laura, whose mouth is parted as she looks over my naked body.

"Now who's staring?" I tease and she jerks, clearing her throat and looking out at the water.

I decide to get it over with and do a little run into the water. The cold liquid prickles at my legs and I have to force myself to run in the rest of the way. It's like being stabbed with needles and I grunt, trying to get used to being submersed in the cold water when it rises up to my chin.

"Be careful," I warn Laura who's watching my reaction anxiously. "Colder than a motherfucker."

"Nice pep talk," She mumbles and I laugh despite myself. I bob around in the water and wait for her as she chews her thumb, still in her underwear.

"Come in already."

"Turn around! You're making me nervous."

I shake my head at her but turn, facing the water instead. The moonlight is sitting patiently above us in the dark sky and illuminating the water, making it appear white just ahead. Everything is so still and quiet, the only sound coming from the water pulsing around me whenever I move. I breathe in the cool air and let it fill my lungs. I think right here, in this moment, is the most peaceful I've felt my entire life.

Laura's screech cuts it all too short.

I wince and turn around, catching the sight of her head dipping under water before coming up. She gasps and swims over to me with her teeth clacking.

"Holy cow, it's freezing! You should have warned me better!"

"I did, baby."

"Did not," She scowls. Her eyes shift over my shoulder and she gasps, seemingly forgetting about her current state. "That's beautiful."

"It is," I agree and turn around again. We both drift in the water and watch the moon above us. I find solace in how large it is and how insignificant it makes me feel. I've always felt like the actions I take in my world are life or death. There has been a constant pressure on my shoulders to be more. Always more. But looking at the moon and how it overshadows me is a reminder that I'm less. It's extremely comforting. It makes me feel human.

"What are you thinking about?" Laura whispers after a moment.

I glance at her, eyes roaming over her face. Her cheeks are red from the cold and her full lips nearly blue. Wet locks frame her face. She is so unbelievably beautiful.

"I'm very glad you made us do this. I didn't think I needed it but...I did. I do."

"Good," She smiles. Her stare travels over me in return and a flash of heat lights up those blue irises that look so vibrant in the dark. I can feel my own blood heating knowing that she's naked underneath this water.

"Need some warming up?" I ask quietly. She takes in an audible breath, nodding just barely. Hell. I push against the water and close the remaining distance between us, pure desire gripping me at the sensation of her bare body pressed into mine. My arms go around her waist to hold her against me and I groan. She feels unbelievable. "Fuck, darlin'."

For as cold as we are, her breath is warm as it skates over me. It makes the desire in my veins grow bolder and I can feel myself hardening despite the freezing water. Laura gasps softly when she feels me against her centre, swallowing hard. I feel her nipples tighten and pebble in response when they brush against my chest. My fingers dig deeper into her waist as a way to ground myself. I am about to lose control, and fast.

"Is this okay?" My throat is full of gravel when I speak.

Laura nods, her arms tentatively sliding around my neck. Unlike mine, her voice is a mere whisper of a sound. "Kiss me."

My lips are on hers as soon she says the words, one hand grasping her head to angle her the way I want. My tongue dives inside the warmth of her mouth to seek out her tongue. They tangle together in slow strokes that make my body pulse with heat. I don't even register the water anymore. I'm burning up from the inside out, feeling an overwhelming need to devour her. All this time I've held back but I don't think I have it in me anymore. I need her, bad.

My hands runs down her body until I'm gripping the back of her thighs. I push against the water to lift her legs and wrap them around me. Laura gasps at the same time I groan when our centres meet flesh-on-flesh. The water ripples around us noisily the rougher we become, kissing with a desperate need. I press my mouth harder to hers, noses crushed and breaths becoming faster, my hips rocking on their own accord. I can feel the way I slide against her so easily because of her slick heat. Water be damned, I know that's her wetness I feel. What I need to fucking know is how it feels to sink into it. Be wrapped up in it. Have it pulse around me when I pound into her and bring her to climax. Fuck.

"Hey!"

We part suddenly and turn in the direction of the voice. There's a flashlight that passes over us for a moment and I squint against the yellow light, lifting a hand to cover my face. It moves to Laura and I blink against the dark, realizing it's a security guard. He's further back where the grass is, which means we can get away.

"Go," I give Laura a little shove toward the sand and start swimming. "Come on!"

"Oh my God!" She giggles and swims with me.

Luckily we stuck close to the shoreline so we're there in seconds and pulling ourselves of the water. I go straight for the gym bag and grab a handful of random clothes, flinging them to her over my shoulder. I grab myself a pair of shorts and quickly slip them on, not bothering with the rest. When I hoist the gym bag up my shoulder and look over it, Laura is dressed only in one of my t-shirts that's long enough to fall mid-thigh. It'll have to do.

"Hey! You can't be here!" The security guard calls.

"Let's go." I grab Laura's hand and take off toward the parking lot. It's harder to run in the sand so we stumble and trip around, running a lot smoother once our feet hit the pavement. My truck is the only car here and we dash for it, barely outrunning the security guard.

We're laughing our asses off by the time we get inside my car and I speed off. The tires screech when I peel out of the parking lot and go for the main road. Only then do we look behind us to confirm it's all clear.

"That was so close!" Laura wipes the tears from her eyes, clutching her stomach. "I think he saw me naked!"

"Me too." My jaw hurts from how hard I'm chuckling myself. "Thank God my cock is impressive or that would have been a lot more embarrassing."

We share a solemn look and then burst out laughing all over again. Laura waves a hand at me in a silent gesture to stop, wheezing out how she can't take it anymore. Instead she turns on the radio and blasts it so we can't say anything to set each other off again. The laughter dies out and is replaced with a comfortable silence as we bop our heads along to whatever is playing. Laura hums softly under her breath and I enjoy listening to it more than the song.

All too soon we're back at her apartment and I turn the radio down as I slow to a stop and face her.

"That was fun." She leans her head back against the seat, watching me.

"I've never done anything like that before," I tell her truthfully. "You were right—it will make a great memory."

She bites her lip in a show of nervousness. "I'm not ready for the night to be over. Do you...maybe want to come upstairs with me?"

I hesitate a moment. Immediately my head starts going through the pros and cons but then I think, why? Why can't I just fucking be with the girl? Why think of all the reasons I shouldn't, when I so clearly should?

I nod in agreement and Laura beams at me, making me more confident in my decision. I find a parking spot and we get out, heading for her apartment. We look like a mess, the both of us dripping with residual ocean water and half-dressed. Luckily it's the dead of night and no one is around so we laugh quietly and quickly step into the elevator.

As soon as the doors close I grip her face and lean down to kiss her. Her small hands go to my torso and she pulls me closer, deepening the kiss when her tongue pushes forward to meet mine. It grows heated within seconds. I'm struck with the reminder of how it felt to have her naked and against me and I can't stop kissing her. Even when the doors open I don't pull away. I keep my lips on hers as I blindly walk us out and down the hall to where her apartment is. We bump into the walls but refuse to separate. We're forced to when Laura has to unlock her door but even then I can't keep my hands away. I wrap my arms around her from behind, my face burying into her neck to suck on the skin there and tasting the salt of the ocean water.

We stagger inside her apartment and Laura locks the door behind her, immediately crushing her mouth to mine again. I waste no time lifting her up and holding her against me to walk her to her room.

The lights are all closed but I remember what her apartment looks like from memory so I find my way easily enough. I drop her on her bed, crawling over her and running my hands over her bare legs. These legs that have driven me out of my mind so constantly. I'm going to see to it that they'll spend the rest of the night wrapped around my neck and torso.

I pull away when Laura pushes against my chest, sitting up on my knees. Without taking her eyes off mine, she peels off my shirt she's wearing and then she's naked. Completely bare to me in the dark, barely visible in the stream of moonlight coming through her window. For a moment all I can do is stare at her. She has little dots of freckles on different places on her body that I want to discover with my mouth and fingers. Her breasts, small, are perky and tight and sit up so nicely they're practically begging to be tasted. Her hips are wider than I expected them to be for her lithe frame but they give her the kind of curves that are driving me insane. The very centre of her is what has my attention and my breaths pick up with the anticipation to be inside of her. I can't look away.

"Is this what you want?" I ask quietly, clenching my fists beside me before I do anything else.

"You are what I want," She whispers back. "More than anything."

My eyes fall shut briefly. Dangerous girl. I will never be the same after this.

I tip my chin toward her, jaw setting. "Your legs. Spread them."

She blinks in obvious shock at first but then complies, spreading her legs for me and giving me a clear view of what I want most. I bring my hand forward to rub a finger along her centre and I find her wet and ready for me already. My brow raises in amusement, more so when she flushes.

"You're the one that kept putting this off," She grumbles defensively and I chuckle under my breath. She isn't wrong. I did keep putting this off but for good reason. I wasn't about to become so involved with someone like her, someone too good for my life. But now I think it could not be more obvious that I can't go forward without her. She's part of me in every way. This happens to be the last part.

I dip my head to run my tongue along her flesh and her light gasp travels to my ears, followed by a soft sigh as her hands thread through my hair to grip me in place. Her taste is as sweet as her and I'm hooked within seconds. I bury my face between her legs as deep as it can go, sucking her clit into my mouth and grazing it with the edges of my teeth. Her hips arch away, like this is too much to take, but she will have to take it.

"Hands," I demand when they start pushing my head back. I don't think she means to do it but it's disrupting me and the way I want to make her fall apart. She gives me her hands compliantly and I lock our fingers together, pinning them down on the bed, and then go back to what I was doing.

"Oh God," She moans when my tongue plunges inside of her. This time her thighs squeeze my head to keep me in place and I smile against her in approval. This will do.

She loses control faster than I anticipate but I have no complaints. Within seconds she's rocking her pussy against my face and chasing release. My groan is deep with satisfaction. I have no doubt I'm enjoying this more than her, having dreamed of doing it for so long.

When her thighs tense beside me I know she's sitting on the edge so I let go of her hands to rub her clit. A few tight circular motions later she shatters beneath me, the sexiest moan tearing out of her as her body quivers and convulses. I take my face away and plunge two fingers into her, spurring her on and wanting her to ride the wave as long as possible. My breaths are frantic as I watch her dig her face into her pillow, her fists bunching up her bedsheets. Shudders continuously wrack through her at my mercy. She is beautiful when she comes.

When her body finally relaxes, she stares up at me through hooded eyes. Her cheeks are flushed, hair splayed around her. I am enamoured.

"Gorgeous." I whisper, swiping my thumb across her lips. She surprises me when she takes it into her mouth and sucks tentatively, tasting herself. It would seem I'm at her mercy now. My chest heaves. "I'm going to fuck you now, darlin'. It will be a far cry from how controlled I've been with you."

She swallows hard, eyes never leaving mine. "Good."

She moves to grab condoms from the drawer beside her and I pump myself, trying to get the pulsing under control. It's been a decent amount of time since I last fucked anyone and even I know I probably won't last too long my first time with Laura. The anticipation alone has been more than I can bear.

She hands me the foil packet and watches raptly as I slide the condom on. I sit up on my knees and grab the backs of hers, opening her legs up to me. With our gazes locked, I sink into her.

Jesus. I abruptly stop because she feels so overwhelmingly good that I might just finish with a few strokes alone. Beads of sweat trickle down my neck from the restraint of holding back and I force my breaths out through my nose. I've never felt such intense, carnal need being inside a woman. It's almost too much.

"Are you okay?" I croak out.

Laura nods, her hips pushing up in a silent plea for more. Her ankles lock at my back and give me the green light I need. I start moving inside of her with controlled thrusts, building us up to the edge. I've experienced all kinds of torture in my lifetime but this might be the sweetest kind. Addicting, even.

"Harder," She whispers, eyes full of lust and pleasure. "Please give me all of you."

Fuck me. I lean over her and draw her knees up higher, opening her up to me wider. The angle changes and Laura moans, head digging back into the bed. I throw one of her legs over my shoulder and start pounding into her, losing all of my restraint. I have no concern for being gentle. There is only her and how I must claim her, consume her, the way she's consumed me.

We ruin each other.

A mess of greedy hands and lips. Pure fucking. I slam into her fast and hard, our hips clashing into each other roughly. When Laura's back arches off the bed I can't resist dipping my head and taking one nipple into my mouth. It looks so inviting, a dusty-rose number, and I suck it deep into my mouth, my hand squeezing her other breast. My large hand easily grabs all of it and I love that I can do that. I love that I can fill her so completely in every way. I bite down on the bud in my mouth and Laura gasps, moaning again when I soothe it with the flat of my tongue.

"I'm so close," She whimpers.

I sit up abruptly and pull out, flipping her onto her stomach and enjoying the back of her as much as the front. I slide my hand over her ass, squeezing. It's marvellous.

"On all fours," I demand.

She does as I ask, breathing heavily as she glances over her shoulder. "So bossy."

"Because it's my job to give orders." I press a hand into the centre of her back, making her arch deeper. Her ass juts out exactly the way I intended and I can feel my eyes blaze with approval. "And when I fuck you, I expect you to follow my orders."

Her breath stutters, surprise flitting through her eyes. For a moment I think I might have gone too far but then she bites her lip, cheeks flushing. "Yes, sir."

It was the perfect thing to say. A growl rips out of me and I slam into her from behind so suddenly that she has to grab the sheets to steady herself. My fingers dig into her hips and my thrusts become rougher, faster, finishing us off. Laura's legs visibly tremble and I know she's dancing on the edge now. I bend over her, kissing along her smooth back until I've reached her neck. I bite hard enough to break flesh and she groans, pushing her ass back against me. My fingers slide to the front of her body until I've captured her swollen clit and I rub as hard as I fuck her. Moments later, her pussy squeezes the entire length of my cock as she shatters.

"Greg!" Her voice is louder than I've ever heard it and my smile forms against her shoulder, knowing I am the cause. "Oh, God!"

"That's it, baby." My fingers don't let up, playing with the flesh of her clit that's doubled in size from her pleasure. I pinch it between my fingers and she cries out, digging her face into the pillows. Her release is so intense I can feel it all over my inner thighs. She is beautiful at my mercy. "That's my good girl."

Her moans are muffled but still such mesmerizing sounds. They undo me instantly and I feel my body lock up when I reach climax. My hips jerks into hers one final time before my own orgasm hits like a motherfucker. I lean over her, locking our fingers together to hold myself up when my body trembles. It's so goddamn intense for a moment I only see red. We finish together and then collapse on the bed, panting hard. Our bodies are stuck together with sweat, the scent of sex heavy in the air, no sounds except for our laboured breathing. Perfect, as I knew it would be.

Laura turns her head to look at me, one flushed cheek laying on the mattress. Locks of hair are matted to her face and I smooth them away, revealing her face to me. Her mouth curls up in a shy smile.

"Worth the wait?" She asks timidly.

I grasp her hand and bring it up to my mouth, kissing her knuckles and oddly wishing I could taste the paint that's usually on them. "You are worth everything."

Chapter 10

"L aura!"

"Greg!" She struggles against the hold of both men, men that have served me in my time as leader. Only now they won't listen to a word I say. "Help me!"

"Don't touch her!" I pull on the rope holding my hands behind my back. "I'll fucking kill you! Get off of her!"

A gun is poised at the tip of her throat and Laura whimpers, eyes going wide. My face drains of blood and fear like I've never known it prevents me from breathing. No.

"This is what happens when you choose a whore over your own family," Father hisses in my ear. "You will not turn soft as long as I'm around, boy. Let this be a lesson."

"Don't do this," I beg. "I'll do anything you want. Father, please!"

He nods at his men and I let out a scream just as the trigger goes off. Laura crumples to the floor, her blood pooling around her like paint on a canvas. It would be poetic if it wasn't so horrifying because it's done. She's gone.

"No!"

"Greg!"

A gasp tears out of me and I sit up, throwing the sheets off my body instinctively. My entire body is a sweating and shuddering mess and I can barely get my breaths under control. Laura's arms go around me and I flinch, still on high-alert from what I now realize was a nightmare. A nightmare so real I can hear the gunshot even now, smell blood in the air. I want to throw up.

"It's okay," Laura whispers and climbs onto my lap. Her arms go around me and she holds me while I shake. Jesus Christ, she's fine. She's alive. Snapping out of it, I crush her to me and hold her like she might disappear at any moment. My face digs into the safe crook of her neck and the way I feel her pulse racing calms me down infinitely.

"I...I thought..." Words aren't a possibility right now. Everything is too overwhelming. I thought she was gone.

"Shh, it's okay. I'm right here." Her arms tighten around me and she kisses my temple. "You're okay. I love you. It's okay."

I barely register her words. My mind is fuzzy with the images of her being shot over and over again. I squeeze my eyes shut and try to think about something else. Like how warm Laura feels in my arms, or how she continues to place soft kisses all over my face, or how she just told me she loves me.

Wait, what?

I pull away to look at her, bewildered. I would not put it past me to have conjured up those words myself. I'm too out of it to be sane so there's a chance she didn't really just say those words. I search her face for a sign that I didn't just make that up.

She smiles at me, hands cupping my face with a tenderness no one has shown me before. "I love you, Greg. I'm not going anywhere."

I didn't make it up. She really did say those words. I swallow hard. "You love me?"

"More than I love painting. More than I love the rain. More than anything, honey." She leans forward to kiss me in a slow and controlled manner. It calms me and maybe that's her intention. She pulls away and sets her forehead to mine. "It's okay if you don't feel the same way. If you're not there yet."

"Crazy woman," I whisper, unable to believe what's going through her head right now. Doesn't she see it—how completely undone she's made me? "You've made me feel more free than I've ever been in my life. You...you make me feel like I'm flying."

A surprised laugh tumbles out of her followed by tears gathering in her eyes. "Flying?"

"Yes." My arms go around her and I hold her warm and bare body against mine. "I'm not falling in love with you, darlin'. I'm flying in love with you."

"Greg," She whispers hoarsely. She closes whatever measly distance remains between us with a tender kiss, one that's slow and full of promise. And I believe her. I believe all the promises she's given me.

What starts as a meek kiss becomes passionate within moments. The pace of our mouths pick up and the heat in my veins boils. Laura shifts in my lap and I groan because I can feel her wetness on my thighs and how she's ready for me. Without another word I lift her up by the hips and sink her down on my cock in one smooth motion.

Laura gasps into my mouth and immediately starts rocking against me. My arm goes around her back to hold her in place as I lay back on the bed and take her with me. Her hair falls around us like a curtain, makes this moment feel even more intimate, and I kiss her harder. The feel of her breasts crushed against my chest and the way her hips lazily lift up and down on my cock are almost too much to bear. I can feel heat spark in my abdomen, warning me that climax isn't far behind.

My fingers slide against her scalp, her hair tangling between my fingers, and I angle her head to kiss her deeper. She moans softly when our tongues slide against each other, riding me faster. I grip her ass and help her move on me, my hips drilling upward and hitting her as deep as I can go. It becomes almost too much and we separate to pull in air. Our foreheads stay pressed together as we both pant through the efforts of our fucking. She feels unbelievable. She feels part of me and not just in a physical sense. She's everywhere all at once and I'm drowning in her.

She places her palms on the bed and pushes up to look down at me. There's tenderness in her gaze as she sweeps my hair back from my face and slides her hand down my cheek. Her hips slow down all of a sudden and her movements become nothing more than leisure rocking. Our eyes stay locked. Even our breaths seem like they're in perfect synchrony. I watch as her pupils dilate every time I push into her, the black dots overtaking her baby blue irises. Her full lips part when I take hold of her breasts and pinch her nipples between my fingers. In return, her palms scrape down my chest and abs and she presses down on them while she shifts her weight up and down on me.

"Oh my God." A breathless cry tears out of her when my thumbs part her pussy and I use the sides of them to squeeze her clit. "Yes."

"Fucking beauty," I murmur, eyeing the way my cock sinks into her only to come out covered with her pleasure each time. I recognize the way her thighs tense from our first time. "Any second now, baby?"

Laura nods wordlessly, biting her lip. I can see the way she's holding her breath with anticipation. I press the pad of my thumb to her clit and draw circles around it while I pump into her. Her pretty tits bounce with each thrust I give her and I can't resist going up on my elbows for a taste. Her moans become louder, frantic, right before she pulses around my length erratically. Her screams are damn near deafening and my lips form a smile around her nipple, sucking harder. The way she squeezes me brings me in right after her and I bury my face in her neck with a deep groan when I feel the tip of my dick pulsing hotly, orgasming into her. It's even better the second time.

We fall back against the bed when it's done in a heap of tangled limbs and sweating bodies. Neither of us makes any move to separate but I don't think we want to. I know I don't. Instead I soak in the way it feels to hold her, the tips of my fingers gliding over her back in lazy circles. Her warmth is grounding and I think I could live in it forever if she'd let me.

"When do you have to go?" She finally whispers. The reminder of what is waiting out there for me is jarring. It taints this moment here and what we just shared. Laura must feel me tense up because she murmurs, "I'm sorry. I just wanted to know how much time I have left with you."

It's a statement that sounds more loaded than it should. It also gets me thinking because how much longer can I do this? I don't want to constantly sneak around and worry about her life being in jeopardy. A good man would leave, let her move on with her life, but I'm too selfish for that. Letting her go is out of the question. The question that poses itself now is what would I give to keep her? What price would be asked of me?

Everything, my mind whispers. Everything you've ever known. Your entire life would be the price. Are you willing to pay?

"Hey." Laura lifts her head, looking down at me worriedly. "Are you okay? I keep saying the wrong things, don't I?"

"No. No, nothing like that. I'm just...thinking."

"About?"

"You," I answer honestly, not wanting to scare her away with what's running through my head.

"No need to think about me if I'm right here," She grins cheekily. My chuckle is immediate and Laura's smile widens as if that was her intention.

I kiss her forehead and pull her head back down to my chest. The ends of her hair tickle my bare abdomen and I breathe in the scent of her shampoo. She's become so familiar to me. How can I leave her behind? But how can I leave my family? I just don't know anymore.

"Do you believe in soulmates?" Laura breaks the silence once again with her quietly asked question.It catches me off guard.

"I can't say I do," I admit, not wanting to lie to her. "I haven't exactly had the best example. My parents were loosely acquainted, if that. I don't think they were ever in love."

She kisses my chest softly and wraps her arm around my waist. "Well, soulmates aren't just supposed to be romantic."

"Then what are they supposed to be?"

"Anything. I think all kinds of soulmates exist. Some souls are meant to be friendships that save you. Some souls make you believe in love. Some souls make you believe in love again when you've lost it. I think there's more than one soulmate for everyone. How can there not be, you know? We're surrounded by billions of people. I think it's up to us to open our eyes and learn from as many of them as possible."

"And what have you learned?" I hang on to her every word, oddly enthralled with the way she sees the world.

"My last foster mother taught me that you can forgive anyone, by taking me in when no other family would. A man in Croatia taught me it's never too late to find your passion, or so he said when he handed me my first paint brush and showed me how to use it. My best friend taught me that everyone deserves a second chance, even after I abandoned her in high school to hang out with losers that I thought would have my back. And you...you've taught me that I'm stronger than I think I am. You've taught me to love so deeply it's hard to catch my breath. So I have four soulmates."

My chest knots painfully at her words. "I'm one of them?"

"Yes." Her voice is a whisper. "Because you changed my life, as all soulmates should."

I don't know what to say. Laura's free spirit has always rivalled my grounded one. I only believe what I was asked to believe. Laura isn't like that. She challenges everything she's been told and sees life the way she wants. If I could be like her, my life would be very different. And I mean that in a good way. Her courage is astounding.

"How do you do it?" I finally ask. "How do you live for yourself?"

She pushes her weight up to look down at me, nothing but sympathy and understanding in her eyes as she her thumb swipes over my lips. "By being selfish. The world will make you believe you shouldn't but only because the world knows how powerful you'd be if you did. Don't let them shrink you, love. You're meant for so much more than you think. It's just waiting to come out and it's one of the things I love about you. I can't wait to see it happen."

"If it happens," I correct softly, shaking my head at her words that are too wonderful for a bastard like me. "You believe in me more than you should."

"You don't believe in yourself enough."

"I'm not who you think I am," I finally grit out. It makes me sick to my stomach that what she sees in me isn't true. She deserves the truth. "Laura, I've killed. I kill. It's my job. Have you ever heard of the South Bloods? I am their leader—a street gang that runs New York's underground crime system. We take care of debts that need to be paid, revenge cases, making money in the most criminal way. People pay with their souls to have us work for them. We are who everyone turns to when they need something illegal done. I oversee all of this and allow it to happen. So please, stop telling me I am good. I am dangerous, especially to you."

I couldn't bring myself to look at her reaction so I stare at the window instead, breathing hard. Part of me feels relief that there are no more secrets but part of me feels dread because I could have handled that better. My stomach bottoms out when Laura sits up suddenly and draws the sheets around her almost protectively. Her back is to me, shoulders tense.

"Shit." I sit up too, wanting to touch her but refrain myself. Have I scared her? "I'm sorry, darlin'. That came out wrong, didn't it?"

There's no answer at first. Without looking at me she finally asks, "So, it's true? What I read in the article when I first met you?"

She's asked me this before. The first time around she had no business knowing the answer but a lot has changed these past three months.

"It's true," I say hoarsely. "I should have told you sooner."

"You should have," She agrees with a whisper. The pit in my gut grows deeper. "But I also didn't push you to tell me because I always had a feeling about what you were caught up in. I just didn't want to admit it to myself."

Fuck, I wish I could rewind time to when I was inside of her and she was whispering that she loved me. How did I lose that so quick?

"Does this change everything?" I ask reluctantly.

She looks at me then, glancing over her shoulder with sad eyes she's clearly trying to fight. No poker face whatsoever, right? "Not everything. I can't help feeling the way I do even knowing the truth. But...it does change a few things. How could it not?"

"I know." I look away, drumming my fingers on the bed nervously. "What does it change for you?"

I hear her sigh before the feel of her warm cheek presses against my shoulder. It takes a lot not to react but I'm grateful that I manage to hold back my relieved smile. "The truth doesn't change my feelings. You're still the man I'm in love with. But I don't know that I can just accept this will always be your life. Even if it's your job and I'm sure you have reasons for...the things you do, I can't pretend it doesn't bother me. And what about every time you walk away and I have no idea of knowing if you'll get hurt? I think you're too good for this life. I think you have to meet me halfway and believe the same if you want this. Us. If you can't then...maybe this as far as we go."

Fuck. She's not really doing this, is she?

"Laura—" I croak.

"Just listen," She whispers and threads her hands through mine. They're so small yet they lend me more strength than I could ever hope to possess. "I know how you feel. I spent years of my life break-ing myself apart to build myself up again and be a better person. But that was only possible because I knew I could do it. If I didn't then we wouldn't be here, Greg. Maybe I would've been a girl on the streets that got caught in the middle of your gang and maybe that's how we would have met. Do you see what a difference it makes when you put yourself first? I can't do that for you. You have to do it for yourself.

Understand that I'm rooting for you but that's as far as I go, baby. The rest is up to you."

I know she's giving me the cold and hard truth. It's the first time anyone in my life has bothered to do that, cared enough to do that. It doesn't mean I don't break out into a sweat at the thought.

She climbs into my lap and holds me and it's only then that I realize I'm trembling. When she kisses my cheek, it feels like goodbye. "I love you. But that's not enough. You have to believe there's a better life for you. Until then I'll wait because you're worth waiting for. It's time to find yourself, okay?"

She starts to sit up and panic grips me, makes it hard to breathe. I grab her waist and hold her where she is, searching her eyes. "Just give me tonight. This night. And then I'll leave."

Her face becomes somber once again and she nods, arms going around my neck. We stay up until the room is bathed in the orange glow of the sun, until we hear the birds chirping, until my phone starts buzzing and reminds me that I can't put this off any longer.

And then I let go.

Chapter 11

My feet pound against the pavement as I sprint, my breaths bursting out of me and lungs burning. Keep going. The sound of a bullet fires off and I duck, picking up my pace. Shit.

Another bullet goes off and I slide across the concrete behind a dump truck. Within seconds I have my gun pulled out from the waistband of my jeans and I click off the safety, shooting to my feet and leaning around the truck so that my target comes into view. I pull the trigger without hesitation. And I don't miss.

"Watch it!" Mitch scowls and drops the shooting board lightening fast. "That could have been my arm, you dick!"

"But it wasn't," I respond evenly. I walk back into view and Mitch hands me the board, the one with a bullet hole right in the centre. He puts his gun away and I do the same, both of us panting. "That's enough training. Let's get out of here."

"Thank fuck," He mumbles under his breath as we head back inside the warehouse. "You take this shit way too seriously. Fucker made me hold a shooting board right next to my body. The goddamn nerve."

"I let you shoot me back so you'd feel safer."

"Right. Safer. I enjoyed being pitted against a killing machine just because I had a glock in my hand."

I chuckle, clapping him on the back in thanks. He's followed every order I've given him and has had my back the way no one else has. He is one of the main reasons I've been able to put my plan together.

It's been three months since that night with Laura and I haven't had a moment's rest since.

I thought a lot about everything she said. I missed her all the time, with no way to contact her. But I know where to find her when the time is right and I've been doing everything to make things right again. If everything goes accordingly, I will be leaving the South Bloods soon.

It was not a decision that came easy. There were too many factors that made it next to impossible. How was I going to keep Laura safe if we were constantly on the run? It's not like I'd be hard to find now that I'm a professional boxer with a direct spotlight under me at all times. Leaving would not be possible without the support of at least a handful of men willing to keep eyes and ears all around to ensure my safety and hers. The only way to turn them was to give them something in return, so I had to plan.

The answer was simple enough—money. But not the kind where I'd throw a wad at them and they'd stay quiet. These men needed a stable source of income if they were going to leave South Bloods to support me. I had to come up with opportunities that would match their respective skills from gang work, something that they would enjoy and pay well. That's when I brainstormed security, selling legal weapons, training, safe-housing, among many others. Quiet spots around the city where ex-members could hide in plain sight and use their job as a security for their own safety. With the money I've made from fighting and leading South Bloods, I've opened all kinds of new locations that are ready to have men moved in. It's coming together slowly but surely.

"I still don't get one thing." Mitch locks the door to the warehouse, the one I've told Father I bought as a new training ground but instead use to devise his downfall. "South Bloods has a law that blood members can't be killed by any and all gangs. Doesn't that make you untouchable so you and Laura would be safe?"

"I'd be safe but not Laura," I explain. "It's blood members only—anyone who directly comes from the Resnick lineage. It's why no one else in South Bloods has protection. It's as selfish a law as the rest of Father's leadership."

"Hell. Here I was thinking you could just marry Laura and give her your name and then you'd both be safe."

"Already thought of that," I shrug. Stark silence greets me and I finally glance away from the whiteboard and find Mitch gaping at me. "What?"

He raises his brows with incredulity. "I meant that sarcastically. You were actually thinking about marrying her?"

"Not thinking. I will." I turn to the board again and look over the names of the men I know would turn with me if given the right motivation. I snap my fingers at Mitch. "Enough gawking. Status updates on the new locations."

He has trouble finding his voice but clears his throat after a brief moment. "Um, three safe-houses closed down on with full payment, one weaponry store sold with complete rights, two gyms in low-income areas for boxing and MMA training, and a handful of security required at each. You're looking at about thirty new jobs."

"Then I'll need thirty men." My eyes scan the twelve I have so far. "Who else?"

"You'd seriously marry her, Raze? You barely know each other." He points out and I sigh, sensing he won't drop it.

"Ask me anything about her then."

He mirrors my stance and crosses his arms. I know he's just worried about me as a friend so I humour him. "Last name."

"Simon."

"Age."

"Twenty-nine."

"Worst fear."

"Dying with regrets. Not having a good relationship with her children if she had any."

"Dreams."

"Owning a gallery of her paintings and one day selling out."

"Something she's never told you but you figured out about her anyways."

"She would like to be a mother. She watches children all the time, especially when they interact with their parents. She wants a girl and she'd name her Emily. I may have read that in one of her diaries."

"I thought you didn't want kids."

"I do if they're hers. Why wouldn't I love more of Laura in this world?"

Mitch finally loses the toughness on his face, his mouth tugging into a smirk. "Better make me best man then."

"Better follow my orders then." I punch his arm, though on the inside I'm pleased of his approval. At least some one does. "Let's finish this."

He groans. "Food first. Would it kill you to feed me while making me do all this secret dirty work?"

My lips twitch reluctantly. "Fine. But something healthy. Part of your training is a good diet."

"Yes, mother." He rolls his eyes and grabs his keys. I follow suit, throwing on a jacket and wiping the board clean before we head out.

Mitch drives so I take the rare free time to collect my thoughts. The truth is I am not sure if I can pull this off. The men who have agreed to work for me could get cold feet and confess to Father. Laura might not want to be with me after all this time. Everything about this is still dangerous. All I know is that it is better than sitting on my ass and wishing for a new life instead of making it happen. No matter what happens, I am going to be selfish. I am going to do better because that's what Laura taught me. And Laura is always right, I've learned.

"Not healthy." I voice my disapproval at the restaurant Mitch pulls into.

"We've been working hard as fuck for months and deserve to kick back a little," He throws back, parking. I may make grown men all around the city shit their pants at just the mention of my name but

Mitch has far since stopped being afraid of me. If anything he's a little too comfortable but I find humour in it.

We walk inside and head for a booth at the back and a waitress is beside us instantly. She eyes Mitch with obvious interest and he notices, putting on a smirk and playing it sweet. I roll my eyes, knowing he's likely to go home with her tonight. In the months I've worked with Mitch one on one and gotten to know him, I've learned he loves women a lot. Too much to ever settle down with one.

She gets our order and walks away with an extra sway to her hips. Mitch doesn't bother hiding his stare that's pinned to her ass.

"You are what women would call a slut," I point out.

He leans back against his booth with a grin. "And as long as they're also calling my name, I don't have a problem with that."

I shake my head. The appeal is not hard to understand. Mitch is what women would consider conventionally handsome. Whereas I'm more on the rugged side, Mitch is more of a pretty-boy. Light brown hair and hazel eyes seem to do it for the women who openly gawk. He also has a nose ring and while I find it punk-ish, women have an appreciation. He once admitted that his dick is pierced—solely for the sake of a woman's pleasure—but I didn't allow him to elaborate on that. Deranged man.

I glance at the counter in the diner to see if our order is ready but find something else instead. Someone, rather. I'm standing up before I even realize with my heart in my throat. Laura.

I should probably stay away. She asked that I leave my life behind and I'm still caught up in it. But I need to see her, to tell her that I'll be there so soon, to ask her if she still wants me after all this time because I never stopped wanting her. Mitch notices too and tries to stop me but it's too late. I walk toward her stool with fast and impatient steps.

She pauses with a fry halfway through her mouth, eyes widening when she notices me. Fuck, I missed those beautiful eyes. "Greg?"

"Darlin'." I wrap my arms around her torso and lift her from her seat, earning her surprised yelp. I should stop but I can't. "You're really here."

I expect her to hug me back, or hope for it at least, but instead she smacks my shoulder and it's not the flirty way she's done before. "Put me down, asshole!"

I immediately set her down on her feet, blinking in shock. This, I was not expecting. "What?"

"Where have you been?" She hits me again and tears gather in her eyes. "You didn't have to outright disappear on me like that! I haven't seen you in months!"

"But...you said..."

"To figure things out for yourself. To push pause on us. But I never meant leave me behind while you did! God, you are unbelievable!"

I have never been so confused. We get a few noticeable stares and I grab her hand, pulling her toward the hallway at the back where the washrooms are. We pass a snickering Mitch and I smack him good on the head for it. Once we're in the privacy of the darkly lit hall, I face Laura again.

"I didn't want to put you in danger. It's a miracle nothing happened to you those three months we were together. I didn't want to risk it until I left South Bloods for good."

She blinks at me, finally simmering down a little. "You're leaving?"

"Yes. You were right—it's not a life I want anymore. I never wanted it but I didn't have the courage to believe I could leave it behind. It's not a simple process and I've been working hard on it so that you could be safe when we'd be together again. If you still want that."

"Of course I do." She shoves my chest, wiping at her face angrily. "I said I would wait but how did I know you would too? You never gave me your number because you said it was dangerous. I don't know where you live or work. You were just gone. I thought you were the one that didn't want this anymore."

"What?" I pull her against me, rocking her when she starts crying into my chest. Hell. I really am an asshole. "I'm so sorry, baby. I didn't think things through. I was just so obsessed with leaving that it didn't even hit me how things would look on your end. Fuck. Forgive me?"

She pulls away again, pushing her hair away from her face. Even red and puffy from the crying, she's so goddamn beautiful it hurts. "On one condition."

"Name it."

"Give me the best apology kiss ever."

My lips crush against hers before she can so much as finish her sentence. I stalk forward until her back hits the wall and then lift her up, guiding her legs around me. She kisses me back just as fiercely, just as hard, and I don't think either of us can breathe right now. But

I don't care. She's my oxygen and I fill my lungs up with the taste of her. I don't know how I went so long without it.

"Wait," She mumbles and takes her mouth away, breathing hard. Suddenly she looks nervous and starts avoiding my gaze. "Are you sure you're going to leave the South Bloods? That we'll be safe?"

"I would never let anything happen to you," I promise. "It's not too long now but I'll leave it all behind. I swear to you."

"Greg," She whispers and closes her eyes. She takes a deep breath. "I'm pregnant."

"What?" I blurt again. That seems to be the question of the day but damn if I can help it. She's pregnant? I look down at her stomach which is completely flat and look back up in question. "You're...really?"

"Yes," She whispers. When her eyes open again I can see the truth in them. Her eyes always tell the truth. "That might have been why I freaked out on you for going AWOL. I wanted to tell you as soon as I found out and I thought I'd never see you again. That you'd never know. I'm sorry."

I set her down, feeling like my mind is spinning. Nothing is making sense right now. There's too many things happening. "We used condoms."

"Just the first time. The second time we were both in the moment. I didn't even realize until you left and I went to shower. I went straight to the nearest drugstore and took a plan B but I guess it didn't work."

"When did you find out?"

"About a month after that night. I missed my period which never happens to me. I knew before I even took the test. I'm coming up on the end of my first trimester."

I swallow hard. Holy fuck, she's right. "And it's mine?"

She glares at me. "I didn't have sex with anyone for over a year before you or since so yes, it's yours."

She doesn't understand. She has no idea why I need to make sure but my mind is spinning with realization. "You're safe."

Her brows crease. "Huh?"

"You're safe," I repeat and sink to my knees. Incredulous laughter escapes me when I cup her stomach and set my forehead to it. "You're untouchable."

"Greg, you're freaking me out. What are you saying?"

"You're untouchable, baby." I look up at her, feeling my throat close in tight with relief. "The blood law. You're carrying my blood. You're untouchable."

She looks like she's losing her patience. "You need to start using words I understand. What are you talking about?"

I curse and get to my feet again, cupping her face. "In South Bloods, there's something called a blood law. Father created it as a way to keep our family safe. Anyone who has Resnick blood is untouchable by any and all gangs. You're essentially safe from any kind of violence and if you break that law, you will be killed. This baby is mine, Laura. It's Resnick blood and you're carrying it. The South Bloods can't touch you which means both you and I are safe. I could leave right now if I wanted."

Understanding dawns on her and eyes come alight with hope. "So...we can be together? It's okay now?"

"They can't touch us. Not my father, not the South Bloods, not any gang. We're safe."

She licks her lips nervously. "Does that mean that you want the baby? Because it's okay if you're not ready to be a father. I get that it's unexpected and I don't want you to think you have to do this."

She still has no idea, does she? "What makes you think I wouldn't want it?"

"I don't know." She ducks her head. "Up until a few minutes ago I thought you didn't want me either."

"That's impossible." I catch her chin and lift it up again. "I want you. Both of you. Hell, maybe after this one we make more. I want all of it if you'll take me back."

She smiles and it's like falling in love with her all over again, just like I did the moment I saw her at my match. "Really?"

"Yes. I just hope that's an Emily in there."

Her jaw unhinges. "How do you know about that?"

"You shouldn't leave your diaries lying around, darlin'."

"Jerk." She smacks my arm with a laugh. "I can't believe you've known this whole time."

"I did, and I love it. I love you. Will you give me another chance to do things right this time?"

She sighs dramatically. "I guess I kind of have no choice, seeing as you knocked me up and all." My unamused glare makes soft laughter bubble out of her. "Kidding, tough guy. We're in this together, okay?"

And I wait for the panic to set in. The fear. The uncertainty. But nothing comes. All I know is I'll do whatever it takes to protect the both of them. My family.

Chapter 12

I burst inside my father's office without warning, confidence urging each step forward. He startles and looks up from his desk, confusion and anger on his face. I take care of both.

"I'm leaving." I waste no time.

"Leaving?" He repeats.

"You will have to find a new leader effective immediately. You're hardly fit to run this gang anymore so my next recommendation is Byron. He knows everything there is to know and can oversee business as I would. I won't be coming back, ever. And if anyone so much as attempts to come near me once I'm gone, don't think I won't use my training to kill them before they even understand what's happening."

He merely stares at me. At least until a loud chortle bursts out of him and he shakes his head as if he's talking to a toddler. My anger increases tenfold. "I've no time for your games, boy. The 5th Street Saints have a business proposal for us. Something about trading members. Their leader will be here in an hour and I expect you to see to it."

I slam my hands on his desk and lean down, seething. "Get it through your head, old man. I am through being leader or having any part in this gang. I have already led them for years against my own will but no more. I have a life to tend to and it has no space for your tyranny."

"Careful. You're scaring me," Father goads with a cruel sneer. "Stop behaving as if you have a choice. What's gotten into you? You will lead this gang for the rest of your life and your sons will lead it after you. This is where we belong. Enough with your delusions."

"Enough with yours! You never gave me a fucking choice! I was a child and you were showing me how to shoot a gun with impeccable precision. You taught me that killing was normal. You made me fight and train until my arms felt like they'd fall off when I should have been kicking a soccer ball or some shit. You conditioned me to become a monster, you sick fuck! I never wanted to be one but I didn't have control over my own life. But now I do and I'm walking away. I will not come back under any circumstance. This isn't my life anymore because I say it isn't. Just try and fucking stop me."

Father stands too, his face contorted with rage. "Where will you go? What will you do? You think you can just move on and pretend the last three decades of your life did not happen? Don't be a child."

"What I do from here on is none of your business. But believe me when I say I'm finally going to live the life I want with the people I want. Consider yourself dead to me."

Father barks out a laugh and puts his hands on his hips. "With the people you want? Don't tell me you're talking about a woman, Gregory."

I have never been more grateful for my ability to keep a straight face through anything. All I want to do is strangle him for closing in on who Laura is but I keep my ground, unblinking. "Don't come after me. You know as well as I do that you can't break the blood law."

"Maybe not for you," He shrugs. "But this woman...I'm under no obligation to protect her. She's putting ideas in your head and I taught you better. I would make a convincing bet that you'd stay right where you are if she wasn't around, wouldn't you?"

My arm shoots out and I grab him by the throat. His breath catches when I dig my fingers in and squeeze as tight as possible. Within seconds he's purple in the face. "You don't touch her. She's carrying my child—your future grandchild. If you touch her then you break the blood law. And once you break the blood law you are no longer protected by it. I would make a convincing bet that your enemies would have you killed within seconds of the blood law being stripped away, wouldn't they?"

I release him and he coughs out in relief, stumbling over and grasping the edge of his desk while he pulls in air. I watch him with a sneer. I should have finished the job while I had the chance.

"You really are despicable," Father laughs, though it sends him into another coughing fit. "Impregnating a woman and suddenly she's untouchable? What a coincidence."

"Whatever helps you sleep at night. But remember if you touch either of us, you are free to be killed by anyone who wishes. Stay the hell away from me, asshole."

"You think it is this easy? This is far from over, Gregory."

"Don't push it!" I swing my arm back and clock him across the face. He stumbles backwards and crashes into the wall behind him, gaping at me in shock. I think until this moment he had no idea how serious I was. "You will not touch my family! I will personally slit your throat and watch the life drain from your eyes if you try it. If anyone tries it. You groomed me to your advantage and today, I've become your downfall. Choke on your failure, Father. Live with it for the rest of your miserable life."

His eyes harden and for a moment he looks like the vicious Abram Resnick that made the South Bloods what they are today. "I am your family, boy. You can run wherever you want but you can never pretend that you don't have my blood in you. I didn't make you anything except what you've always been."

"Then why are you experiencing fear? I can see it in your eyes, old man. I see right through you and I'm not impressed."

"This is a mistake," He spits. "You will regret it. You should know the consequence of making me your enemy."

"The only consequence I've faced at the hands on you is all the blood I'm responsible of spilling. Anything that comes after that will pale in comparison. I do not fear you, nor do I care for you. You lose."

His nostrils flare and he takes one step forward. "So be it. Don't say you weren't warned."

"Remember those words if you find yourself dying at my hands."

"To hell with you!" He shouts at my retreating back. Fuck him. I never want to see the bastard again.

I'm not surprised when I leave the warehouse and find the majority of the South Bloods loitering around. I have no doubt that they heard my argument with Father and when they see me, they all stiffen and face me expectantly. It is hard to tell what they want to hear right now.

"What was that, Raze?" One of them finally breaks the silence with his haughty demand. "You're fucking leaving?"

"We're hearing rumours," Another calls out. "That you're doing all of this just for a girl."

"You've gone soft!" Someone in the back shouts and the men cheer out their agreements, all their rage directed my way. "You're leading the most ruthless gang in New York and you're stepping down for a woman? It's a fucking disgrace!"

"We don't leave our men behind!" The accusation is followed by another round of cheers. The crowd of men gradually get closer to me, openly sneering and glaring. "We want to see consequences, Raze! Who have you chosen over your own men? Don't think we won't come after you!"

"And do what?" I ask. My voice is calm and low. They are all feeding off each other's testosterone, flooding their lungs with false courage and forgetting where they stand in our hierarchy. Either I can panic or make an example of their disobedience. "Remember the blood law."

One man steps forward. Duke. I've worked with him for nearly a decade now and he has always followed orders. Although he has a temper that runs hot and is one of our more ruthless members.

He has done things even I cannot stomach, but I stay on my side of business and let him stay on his. Until he steps into my face now, shoulders pushed back under the false guise that he has the upper hand here. It's only because our men cheer for him and his mouth curls with bravery. Idiotic man.

"I would think leaving your men behind means breaking the blood law. And once the blood law breaks, you have no protection." He cracks his head side to side, grinning wolfishly. "Where are you hiding the pretty little thing anyway? Must have one hell of a pussy to make the great Raze fall to his fucking knees. Maybe I should go see for myself what all the fuss is about."

An example I will make.

The men behind him fall into fits of laughter and call out similar remarks. Duke juts his chin out proudly, chest knocking into mine. We are almost the same both in height and muscle but he does not know how to use his body to kill like a machine. I do. And right now, I don't hear or see or feel anything beyond the words he just said. I shut down, honing in on my rage to charge myself up on the inside. On the outside I'm stoic and Duke mistakes it for fear.

"What was that?" My question is spoken quietly but loud enough that the rest of my men hear. They finally simmer down, openly buzzing with anticipation to see what will happen.

Duke's grin widens. "I said, where are you hiding that piece of ass? I'm going to show her how a real man fucks, whether she's willing or not."

Breaths levelled, in and out. Feet gradually widening into stance. Hand already reaching for the knife in my pocket. But he sees none of this because he is a blind man. All he sees is the face I put on, cold and unblinking. I nod. "One more time, Duke. One more."

Duke chuckles. He's drunk on courage and uncaring that he's leaving his fate up to me. And I decide he will not live to see another minute of his life.

"I think I heard her name somewhere too." He licks his lips, eyes flashing. "Laura?"

Dead man.

Before he can blink, the heel of my palm strikes into his nose to catch him off guard. It was not meant to harm, but to distract. And while he's processing the burst of pain with a dazed look, I jam my fingers into his mouth and yank his tongue out. My knife slices it off in one smooth motion.

A tortured howl erupts from him and he falls to the floor, screaming in pain. Bursts of blood erupt from his mouth and he keels over, hand covering his face to try and salvage the mess made of him. It's pointless. He bleeds out all over the cement he lays on, cries tearing out of him. My face doesn't budge an inch.

I face my men and they all stumble backwards, growing somber once again and remembering their place. I hold Duke's tongue up before tossing it at them. "This is for speaking to me with disrespect. He is not the only one who talked out of his ass so who would like to go next? Who would like to challenge their leader?"

I get no response. My brows push up. "What's wrong? Weren't you all about to enlighten me of the consequences I'd face for leaving? Finish it. Tell your leader what you think you can do to him. I could use a laugh."

Still no response. I point to Jett, the man who claimed he'd come after me. "Get up here."

The men around him move back and open a pathway from him to me. Jett laughs nervously. "Raze..."

"Get up here!" I take my gun out of the waistband of my jeans and point it at him. "You do not disobey me!"

Jett panics, eyes darting around. He tries to stand tall, pride preventing him from owning up to the grave mistake he made. "I was just voicing what everyone was thinking! You—"

I pull the trigger. The bullet hits him neatly between the eyes and he falls to the floor. Before his body can even make contact with the cement, I turn to Duke and lift him up by the collar. His shirt is drenched in blood, face smeared, and he whimpers because he is unable to say anything. I have no mercy for him and the things he implied he would do to my Laura. Bastard. I poise the gun inside his mouth where his tongue should be and shoot. The bullet goes through the back of his neck and I drop him again, letting him bleed out like the miserable man he is.

"Let me clarify one thing." My voice sounds monotone. Robotic. I simply pocket my gun again and grab the man closest to me, tauntingly wiping my bloodied knife across his neck. He gulps hard. "Every single one of you could ambush me at once. You could step forward with guns blazing. But you would all end up dead at my feet even then. Who can tell me why?"

Still no answer. Pathetic men. Raving and bragging about being the most ruthless there was, yet fall silent from the child's play I just demonstrated. My eyes harden with warning.

"I may be Abram's son, but I am your leader because I have no rival. No equal. The status we have in this city is because I am the face of South Bloods. You are all thriving off my legacy. So don't fucking tell me that I never did anything for you. I have kept each and every one of you alive by choice. Let Duke and Jett be proof of that. And make no mistake—I am not soft. I do not hesitate to kill. If any of you tries to come after me or harm my family, the woman carrying my child, I will torture you until you beg for death. The blood law may offer protection, but none of you would have a chance even if it didn't. If you think otherwise, come face your leader right now and prove me wrong."

Wary glances are passed between each other. A lot of them are directed behind me and when I glance there, I find Father standing and glowering. I silently dare him with my eyes to approach me. I've long since outmatched him and he knows it. He might put up the most decent fight from anyone in this gang but he won't win. I turn around when it becomes clear he won't step up.

"I may be leaving but I am still your leader. You will always answer to me. I could come back decades from now and your sons and daughters will all know my name and the work I've done. They will fear me just as you do. This is my fucking kingdom. God help the fool who ever tries to fight me for my throne."

And I leave it at that. Without another word I stalk away, kicking Duke's lifeless body to the side. I lock eyes with Byron who's face is as passive as mine but there's a certain pride in his eyes that cannot be mistaken. He might be the only one I will actually regret leaving behind.

"If anyone wishes to join me, they can." I'm reminded to call over my shoulder. "If you do not wish to continue gang work then you may join my business. We could use the skills some of you possess. You decide what life you want to live just as I have. Approach me with respect and I will show you mercy."

Then I leave it behind for good. It is the first time I've been able to breathe in years.

Chapter 13

Intuition is the most important skill a leader can have. You can have everything else but if you don't have intuition, then your leadership will fall short. In the world I grew up in, intuition is life or death.

That's why, as I help Laura carry her boxes from her apartment to the moving truck, I listen to that twist in my gut that has been bothering me for the past couple of hours.

There's essentially no reason to be feeling this way. Months have passed and I have not heard a peep from the South Bloods. Mitch and the few men who have joined my business around the city have kept their eyes and ears open but no one has tried to follow me or approach me after the day I left. It has been quiet and while I was wary in the beginning, I gradually learned to accept the past was past. But this feeling in my gut now is what has saved my life on multiple occasions so I listen.

"Baby," I call for Laura as she waddles over to me. She's nine months along and her belly is bigger than she is. I have no idea how someone as tiny as her is carrying what seems to be a very big baby. Oh, and we were right—it is an Emily in there. "I'm going to drop you off at Mitch's place for a couple of hours, okay?"

"Why?" She pouts. She's become very needy in her final trimester but I'm enjoying it. If there is one thing I miss about being a leader it's taking charge. It has been far too long since I felt productive and taken lead on something so I've been smothering Laura and doing everything for her. She's been extra emotional and affectionate the past couple of months so it's worked out well.

"I'm going to go check on a few things," I answer vaguely.

She perches her hands on her hips. "Be more specific than that, Greg. I know that tone and I don't like it."

I sigh and close the remaining distance between us, cupping the back of her neck. "I'm going to go to the South Bloods headquarters."

"What?" Her thumb flies to her mouth in her usual show of worry. "Why would you do that? Something bad could happen."

"That's exactly why I need to go," I explain calmly. I take her thumb out of her mouth and bring her hand to my lips instead, kissing the smudges of paint. "Something is bothering me. I don't know what but I trust my feelings."

"Is it a bad feeling?"

"Yes. I can't seem to shake it and I'd rather be safe than sorry."

She nibbles on the corner of her lip. Over the past few months I've slowly told Laura all the gory details of my life, leaving out the ones that she shouldn't know. Some sins you are meant to take to your grave and indulging Laura in them does not help anyone. She knows more than enough to know who I truly am now and though she seemed surprised and wary at first, she learned to understand that a lot of my life was dictated despite my actions being mine. She understands what my life once was which is why she's visibly freaking out that I'm going back. Instinctively it seems, her free hand cups her belly protectively.

"Don't...don't get hurt, okay? Be as careful as you possibly can and don't stay there a second more than you need to." She swallows hard, trying to put on a smile. "I can't lose you, love."

"Nothing will happen," I assure her. "I just need to make sure everyone is following my orders of staying away. I can't lose you either, right?"

She nods and pulls in a breath. "I know. I'm sorry. Let's just blame it on the hormones."

She manages a small smile but her eyes flood with tears. I curse and pull her to me, hugging her as best as I can with her stomach between us. I stroke her hair while she sniffles into my chest. She is an unbelievably strong woman for putting up with me. Not everyone would have the courage of choosing a partner with a past like mine, a past that never really goes away and ultimately puts her and Emily in danger, but still she chooses me. Her bravery has always been what drew me in and that hasn't changed at all.

"I'll be fine," I promise. "I could never leave my two girls behind, darlin'. I just need to do this one thing and then we're out of here."

"And we'll be safe in Boston?" She asks in a small voice.

My finger slide up into her hair to tug her head back gently. I make sure she's looking me in the eye when I say, "Turf gang violence is limited to the city it's in. Being in a new city and having the blood law on our side makes us practically invisible. It's time to start a new life. I promise this is the last time I'm going to drag you down."

"You never drag me down," She whispers. "You help me fly. Everyday I fly in love with you."

"I flew first," I whisper back and lean down to take her lips between mine. I kiss her with as much assurance as I can and her grip tightens on me in return. When I feel a little wave of movement on my abdomen, I pull back with a chuckle and crouch down. My hand splays across Laura's belly. "You too, darlin'. Daddy loves you so much. I'll be right back, okay, Em?"

Another kick. I smile and kiss Laura's stomach before standing up to kiss her once more. She strokes my cheek. "Be safe. If I don't hear from you in two hours I'll go bat-shit crazy. You know I have it in me."

"You terrify me," I respond sombrely, her laughter encouraging my own grin. "Mitch is in the truck. Stick with him."

She nods and watches as I jog over to my car. I get in and reverse, heading toward the intersection. Laura blows me kisses until I turn left and am out of sight. That's when my easy smile finally drops.

I'm on high alert the drive over, my fingers drumming the wheel. Maybe I will get there and nothing will have changed. But maybe this feeling is here for a reason and I won't like what I find. I double check my glove compartment and take out both guns, strapping them to my waist at the next red light. Then I put on a pair of sunglasses and hat to avoid being noticed. I still attend several matches fighting professionally and am starting to get recognized in public. The last thing I need is for the media to catch me heavily equipped and start digging into information about me. I don't need anyone finding out about Raze. He's dead for good now and I would like it to stay that way.

The familiar streets leading to our warehouse flips a switch inside of me. I've learned to be a better person but that doesn't mean I'm naive enough to have my guard down around here. In these streets, being a killer is the only way to stay alive and I'll be damned if I let anyone see even a smidge of weakness from me.

I park my car and immediately know something is wrong. There's usually background chatter or some kind of energy buzzing around the streets of our turf. Right now there is only silence and I don't like it.

I take one of my guns into my hand before getting out of the car. I raise the gun up, slowly stalking to the warehouse while my eyes dart around. So much fucking stillness. Why? I force myself to cool down and think straight. This could be an ambush for all I know and I need to remember my training. Isolate my senses—ears honed in on the sounds behind me and eyes straight ahead so that no one catches me off guard. I use my booted shoe to nudge the door open quietly and step inside. There's a metallic tinge in the air and I know it all too well. My nostrils flair with familiarity. Blood.

"Father?" I call out. My voice echoes off the steel walls. "Byron?"

Something clatters up ahead. I click back the safety on the gun and point in the direction of the noise. A few seconds tick by of total silence so I walk toward it instead, my finger on the trigger. I add the slightest bit of pressure, ready to pull, but stop short when I recognize one of my members propped up against a garbage can and bleeding out from the gut.

"Finn." I immediately crouch down and grip his lolled face, tilting it up. "What the fuck happened?"

"Raze," He groans, barely able to get his eyes open. "Ambush."

"Ambush? Who did this?"

"V-Vice Lords."

I feel myself lock up. "Not possible. They are too pathetic to pull off an ambush. Somebody helped them."

He gurgles out a laugh but there's nothing humorous about it. "They c-came for you. Something about a debt?"

"A debt?" I scowl. "I didn't purchase shit from them. Turned their deal down."

"So we heard." He coughs violently, folding over. Another groan tears out of him. "The rest are at the b-back."

I frown and follow his line of sight but I don't see anything. Something isn't right here. My jaw locks and I turn to Finn again, grabbing his throat and squeezing hard. He sputters in shock and visibly claws for air.

"Let's try this again," I start, pure menace lacing again. "And this time tell me what Father is up to back there or I'll finish you off myself."

His eyes widen and I loosen my hold enough for him to talk. "I am t-telling the truth! All of our members are injured!"

I squeeze tight again. "You are only digging your grave deeper, Finn. Ambush or not, I know Byron is leader and he is too skilled to take a hit this bad. The truth or your life—which do you want to give up?"

He holds his hands up. "Don't! He made me! Sh-shot me and said he'd only get me help if I told you this lie!"

"Better." I nod and drop him. I will spare him his life, but he can live with his wounds for attempting to betray me. It is his own doing if they kill him eventually.

I draw my other gun from my waistband and click the lock back on it too. I hold them both in front of me, breathing evenly as I approach the back of the warehouse. I don't step outside but I do teeter on the edge and debate my next steps. If this really is an ambush then I can't expect to win unless someone has my back. I should have brought Mitch with me. Fuck.

"Father," I bark. Both my fingers settle over the triggers of my guns. "I wouldn't recommend doing anything stupid right now."

A shot goes off and I duck, barely dodging the bullet that hits the wall behind me. I move behind a large crate just as another shot is fired at me, cursing. So this is how it's going to be? I lean from behind the crate and angle my gun, pressing the trigger. Father disappears from sight just in time and I use the crate to shield myself once more.

"Don't do this!" I yell. "You're breaking the blood law!"

A bullet whizzes through the crate and splinters of wood break apart over my head. I cover myself with my arms just as jagged pieces fall down on me. Another bullet hits the crate beside me and I flinch because one more inch over and that would have been my head. It's almost like the shot was missed on purpose. I peer to my right where Byron is stationed, standing further back on the walkway. His expression is grim and full of warning. I'm not going to make it out alive if I stay here.

I push my weight up and sprint for the front of the warehouse. I can hear heavy steps behind me and pick up my pace, lungs burning as I head for the door. A shot fires just to my right and I duck, keeping low and moving as fast as I can.

"Come around the other side!" I hear Byron's command. "I got him!"

Shit. Running is not going to help. I get low and slide across the floor until I'm behind a pile of boxes. Without hesitation I shoot at Byron who is only a couple of steps behind me. He curses and ducks, eyes locking with mine and running straight for me. I pull the trigger again, clocking him in the arm. He grits his teeth with a deep groan but pushes forward until he's tackling me to the floor. He swings a punch to my face that snaps my head to the side and another jab to my gut. I am undeterred as I throw my weight to the side and roll us over so I'm on top, my right cross decking him in the jaw. My arm swings out for another punch and the crack of flesh on flesh bounces off the metal walls. I dodge his arm when it shoots up, my knuckles meeting his eye socket.

"Stop!" He hisses, flinching away. "Bastard! Listen to me for a second!"

"If you think you can kill your leader you are sadly mistaken," I seethe, my next punch coming down on his nose.

"Listen!" He barks and kicks me off, once again on top. His hand grabs my throat and I struggle against his hold to breathe, squirming. Byron's eyes blaze with anger and...panic. "There isn't much time, Raze. Listen to me."

What on earth is he talking about? I finally stop struggling and Byron lets go of my throat tentatively, hands up as if he's waiting for me to start fighting again. I don't. He nods when he believes I'm going to stay down.

"You weren't supposed to come here," He starts, shaking his head slowly. "I don't know how you did it but you knew to come here instead of going home. It fucked everything up."

"Fucked what up?" I demand.

"We had to improvise. Make it look like an ambush and kill you in the crossfire instead. We've had eyes on you for months and knew you were leaving the city with Laura. We tried to kill you before you left but fuck, you came here instead. How did you know?"

"Know what? Say it as it is!"

Something like regret flashes through his eyes. "We set a bomb at Mitch's house. We knew you were headed there. It's wired to go off as soon as the front door opens. By some miracle you came here instead so we had to improvise a different way to kill you. But it's likely Mitch and Laura are not alive right now."

No.

No, no, no.

My stomach sinks, a pit so deep that I feel hollow on the inside. I can feel the way my blood drains from my face with pure fear. Mitch. Laura. Emily. My family. They killed my family.

An in humane sound rips out of me, so guttural and tortured and hollow that Byron flinches. My arm swings out with so much force that I hear the way his jaw snaps when my knuckles make contact with his face. Byron'a deep groan is laced with misery as he falls off me and clutches his face, eyes pinched shut from the pain. But it is not good enough. I grab his face and then I don't stop. Punch after punch after punch until he's bloody and unrecognizable. Face swollen in size. I only stop because I have to go to them. I have to know if they are gone.

"Go around the back," Byron groans when I start to take off. I look down at him, still breathing hard from the brute force I used on him. His words are slurred through his lips that are double in size and flooded with streaks of blood. "I told them to come out front. Go around the back."

My brows crease together. He is helping me? But he is also responsible for that bomb, for not warning me and saving my family. I shake my head and head for the back. Even the good men of South Bloods are monsters. I should have left sooner.

As soon as I round the warehouse, I hear the sound of a gunshot right before pain bursts through my upper shoulder. A scream tears out of me and I go down, my body slamming into the cement and scraping my face. It feels like my entire body was doused in gasoline and lit on fire. I groan, turning my head with more effort than I thought I needed and gritting my teeth at the sight of blood. This was a calculated shot. Enough to hurt me gravely but not enough to kill me. This is the kind of shot that makes a man teeter on the edge of life and wish death could kiss him so he no longer feels pain. This is a torturous shot and one I know all too well.

"Fuck you," I spit on the boots that stop in front of me, already knowing who it is.

"Didn't I tell you you'd regret this?" Father crouches down. His face is wicked and then he digs his finger into my bullet wound, igniting a fresh burst of pain that makes it feel like my lungs are collapsing. Another scream is wrenched from my mouth. "No one disobeys Abram Resnick, least of all his own fucking son. This wouldn't be happening if you had just remembered your place and done your job."

"You are a miserable man," I manage to bite out. "So driven by your own greed that you are willing to kill your own son. You killed Mother and now you're going to kill me. Don't talk to me about regrets when your entire life has been a joke."

"I did not kill your mother!" He screams in my face, breathing hard. Something passes across his eyes and if I didn't know any better, I would say it was pain. "I didn't think she was capable of taking her own life."

"But she did. And you didn't think I was capable of leaving South Bloods but I did. You can't control everything, Father. For once in your fucking life make the right choices. Are you really going to look me in the eye and kill me?"

He hesitates, gun poised at my throat. I watch as a million thoughts visibly run through his mind and he is unable to look away from me.

"What's happening?" Someone behind us shouts. "I thought we weren't going to let him live!"

"Finish him, Abram! He betrayed us!"

"Let there be consequence!"

And like a switch, Father's eyes harden once again and he clicks the off the safety. Miserable, miserable man. He's really going to do it.

"The blood law—" I try one last time.

"But I didn't kill you," He shrugs. "We were ambushed as far as New York is concerned. And the South Bloods are willing to keep this quiet if it is your head at cost. You betrayed your men. You betrayed me, son."

"You betrayed me first," I hiss, disgusted. "By never being my father a day in my life. So kill me. Fuck the law. We are not blood."

Another wave of emotions passes through his eyes at my words but I don't want to see it. I pinch my eyes shut with anticipation, waiting for it to end. I apologize over and over to Laura and Emily and Mitch and hope they are alive. Hope they can forgive me if they are not.

The gun is fired.

Chapter 14

I wait for the pain but it doesn't come. Only my shoulder continues to pulse from my wound that was already there. Did Father miss?

I open my eyes again, jerking at the sight of his body on the floor beside mine and bleeding out. Confusion immobilizes next for a few moments but just as quick it is replaced with sinking dread.

"Father?" His eyes are open, soulless. My heart pounds faster. "Father? Father!"

No answer. A thin line of blood trickles from his mouth. My eyes run all over him in panic until I spot the source of a wound. A bullet to the chest sitting neatly between his lungs. It is the skill of a true marksman and I know of no one in this gang beside myself that could take such a shot.

"He broke the blood law." A deep voice calls for my attention and I look to the right, at a man with a rifle strapped to his chest. He's leaning out the window of a car, absentmindedly chewing a toothpick. "That was our shot to take. Been wanting to kill the bastard for far too long."

"Where did you come from?" I demand. I struggle to get to my feet, grunting at the pain that shoots up my arm when I stand. Blood continues to seep out of me and I know I need help. "How did you know to be here? Who are you?"

His lips pull back in a sneer. "We heard rumours that you left your gang, Raze. Thought I'd keep an eye on your old man and see what he would do next. That's the difference between the two of you—Abram always acted on violence alone. You? You're a smart motherfucker. Absolutely lethal and crazy intelligent. It's why no one fucks with you. Abram was always the easier target."

"I don't need a fucking bedtime story and pat on the back," I spit. "You killed my father. You better have some fucking answers for me."

"Your father is a messy leader," He shrugs, continuing to chew his toothpick and casually leaning outside his window. "South Bloods haven't been doing so hot since you left and every street gang knew it. They were too excited to witness the downfall but I wanted a hand in it."

"Why?"

He grins. "Because I want to be on top now. The Asesinos deserve to be the best."

"You're their leader," I finish for him, catching on. I shake my head and fight the urge to pass out. I'm no doctor but I've been in enough fights to know when I've lost too much blood. I need to get help and I need to know if my family is still alive. "I'm out of here."

"We didn't know about the deal our men cut with Lloyd," He calls when I start to turn around. "The ambush—we didn't know. You were betrayed my your man and we were betrayed by ours. Think what you want about the Asesinos but I'm a good leader and I wouldn't pull shit like that."

I glare. "You killed my father!"

"He was about to kill you and you know it!" He shouts back. "You're lucky Ive been following him around and knew this was going down today. I saved your life."

"Out of the goodness of your own heart, right?"

"Fuck that, Raze. I'm a good leader because I do good business. You're in my debt now. If the Asesinos ever need help from South Bloods, your gang better step up."

"Nice," I mutter. But he is right and we both know it. I'd be dead if he didn't intercept in time.

I look at Father's body with a tight throat. I hated him until the very end but I never wanted to witness his death like this.

I quickly look away and pull out my phone, cursing at its state. There's cracks everywhere but it still works and when I get it open, my stomach sinks at the number of missed calls from Mitch. I call him up with shaky hands, dread making it hard to breathe. Relief like I've never known it slams into me when he picks up. "Mitch."

"Where the fuck have you been!" He shouts. "Laura—"

"What happened? Where's my girl? Tell me she's alive, Mitch." I beg.

"Alive?" He sounds floored. "What the fuck are you talking about?"

What? I'm so goddamn confused. "I thought when you went home—"

"We didn't make it to my place. Laura started getting really bad contractions so I turned around and went to the hospital. She's fucking crowning. The baby is coming."

I'm grateful for the sturdy pile of crates behind me that catch me when my body goes limp. Holy shit. Holy fucking shit. They never made it home. The bomb never went off. They're alive.

"Hello? What the fuck is going on? Get your ass here now! Your daughter is about to be here any minute! We're at the hospital on 3rd."

"Be right there," I croak.

I end the call and an incredulous laugh escapes me, followed by a wave of tears. My family is still alive. By some miracle, none of us made it home to that bomb. Good fucking riddance.

I push off the crates and start for my car, fighting the agonizing pain shooting up my arm. I can't fucking drive like this.

"Need a ride?" Fucker chews on his toothpick expectantly, brows raised. I scowl but fuck, I don't have a choice here.

"Fine."

I get in, crying out without meaning to when my weight shifts. Something doesn't feel right. My shoulder feels detached or something.

"Needs to be popped back in," He confirms. He throws his rifle in the backseat and faces me, grabbing hold of my arm. I hold my breath in anticipation and the fucker smirks like he's enjoying this. "Big girl panties, Raze."

"Just do it before I blow your head off," I snap. "Deal or not, you'll always be my father's killer. Stop trying to play nice."

That sobers him up. He nods and without another word, pops my shoulder back in place. I bite down on the collar of my bloodied shirt to muffle my scream, a fresh wave of dizziness slamming into me.

"Raze? Shit."

Blackness dots my vision and I try to blink it away but it's a fight I lose. I feel my consciousness slipping away, and part of me is relieved. Part of me feels at peace. So I let myself go.

The sound of a gunshot sends a bolt of electricity up my spine and I jerk, gasping as I come to.

I immediately groan when another burst of pain shoots out at my shoulder, making my arm feels like it weighs a ton. I sink back into the bed and look around with groggy eyes. At first I look for the shooter but then I remember I was dreaming about Father being shot. The reminder brings back a flood of memories, specifically one. Laura. Emily.

I sit up again and this time I ignore the pain. Shit. I need to go see them. I need to go hold my girls, damn it.

I stagger to my feet, softly wheezing through the enormous pain pulsing everywhere. I feel like I was fucking body checked by a bus. It's hard to catch my breath and I pant as I yank away the wires attached to me. At that moment a nurse walks in and gasps, abandoning her clipboard and rushing over to me.

"Mr. Resnick, stop! You're still recovering from surgery! Please lie back down before you make your injuries worse."

"Get off," I mumble when she grabs my arm. "I'm serious, let me go. I need to go."

"Calm down," She tries again. "What is it that you need? I'll get it for you."

"My family!" I snap, chest heaving with panic. "I need my family! I...I had a baby girl. I think. I don't know where they are. Fuck. Please let me go."

"Sir, please." The nurse holds her hands up. "You don't need to go anywhere. You were admitted in the same hospital as your partner. Umm...Layla?"

"Laura," I correct, hope flaring.

The nurse nods enthusiastically. "That's her. She delivered the baby a few hours ago. Just please lie down and I'll go get them. You woke up sooner than you should have and fought off the dosages given to you. You're going to have to relax or you won't recover."

"Just please get them." I lie down on the bed again and the strains in my muscles go away. The nurse quickly attaches my IV before trotting off.

The seconds feel like fucking hours as I stare up at the ceiling. Anxiety like I've never known it slams into me from all corners. Usually a father has time to process when he's become one but I didn't. One second Laura was pregnant and just like that the baby was here. I just became a dad and I had no idea. The nurse said Emily was delivered a few hours ago and I had no idea. Already I'm the shittiest fucking father. The urge to just scream in frustration is overwhelming.

There's an irritating squeaking sound and I glance at the door just as Laura is wheeled inside my room. She has a bundle in her arms and my chest twists at the sight of both of them. They both look okay from what I can see. I try to sit up but that damned nurse is beside me lightening quick, ushering me to stay in bed. I reluctantly listen but only because my eyes meet Laura's and the silent way she gestures for me to stay put.

"Hi darlin'," I whisper when Mitch parks her wheelchair next to the bed, putting the stopper on. He sighs heavily and watches me with a grim and tired expression, offering the faintest smile. I nod back in acknowledgement and thanks.

"Are you okay?" Laura asks softly, eyes grazing over me. Her eyes are watery. "God, I thought I lost you. I was so scared."

"I thought I lost you," I croak back. Laura leans forward and presses her mouth to mine gently. I kiss her back, the relief I feel making it hard to breathe.

When we pull away I can't help glancing down and my breath catches at the sight of her. My daughter. She is as gorgeous as her mother and I am enthralled, unable to look away from those blue eyes and the way they watch me. I hesitantly life a finger and let it rest on her cheek. My throat locks up when her nose does that little twitch like Laura's.

"Meet Emily," Laura whispers with a grin. The nurse helps me sit up against the pillows and Laura hands our daughter to me. I panic at first. She's so small and I am afraid that I'll hurt her somehow. But then Laura takes a seat beside me, helping me figure out how to hold her. Emily continues to stare at me with eyes just like her mother's. Laura strokes her head. "That's your daddy, baby. Say hi."

I'm grateful that the nurse and Mitch have left the room to give us privacy because a wave of emotion hits me suddenly. It might be the first time in my life I've cried and shudders wrack through me from the intensity of it all. No matter how hard I try I can't calm down.

"Love?" Laura asks worriedly when I gasp for air between sobs. Her arms go around my neck and she pulls my head down to bury it in hers. I cry into the crook of her shoulder uncontrollably. "Hey, hey. What's wrong? Shh. It's okay, baby."

"It's not," I barely manage to say. "I ruined everything. I-I wasn't there for you. I missed her birth. You did this all by yourself. It was all my fault."

"What?" Laura hugs me tighter. "Baby, what are you blaming yourself for? Don't say that."

"I should have been there for both of you. You-you deserve so much better. Fuck. I'm so sorry."

Laura crushes me to her even harder if possible and when she speaks, her voice sounds thick with emotion. "You listen to me right now, Greg. You are exactly what Emily and I deserve. You flipped your entire world upside for us. You left your whole life behind for us. You sacrificed everything for us. If there's one thing you've always been, it's there for us. You might not have been there for the birth but you were fighting to save us both. You are the reason we're alive."

"But I'm also the reason you are always in danger. What kind of father am I? I'm just like my own and look at where that's gotten him."

"Where?" Laura asks with obvious confusion.

Another wave of sadness slams into me. I didn't realize how much I am actually grieving for him. "He's dead. He tried to kill me and then...then he got shot. Look at what he did to himself, Laura. I lost my father long before he died. What if I do the same thing to Emily?"

"Your father died?" Laura gasps. "Oh my God. I'm so sorry, Greg."

"Me too," I whisper and it's the truth.

"Greg, listen to me. You have never been like Abram a day in your life. Even when you were working for him and following his commands, your heart always knew what was right. You make good choices. You made our beautiful daughter and she's proof of that goodness. We are so lucky to have you and we choose you, baby. You're always going to be the one I choose."

My eyes fall shut. How is it that she can love me like this even after everything I have put her through? I look at Emily again, who is sleeping soundly with a little smile on her face, and hug her closer. Hug Laura closer. Because when you've lost everything, you should hold the people that remind you what it's like to be alive.

"This time we're free. This time I mean it. I'm never going to let my past ruin your life again," I promise.

Laura shakes her head at me. "Everybody has a past. And your past made you who you are today, even the bad parts. You might hate what your life once was but I don't because it brought you to me. That's all that matters."

Hell. I kiss her again, and when she smiles against my mouth I know I'm going to be okay. That we are going to be okay. Because that's what Laura does—she saves me.

"I love you," I nip her mouth before pulling away.

Her grin widens. "Flying in love with you, babe."

I chuckle under my breath, holding Emily against my chest and sighing in relief. "I flew first."

Epilogue

8 years later...

"Oh, God," Laura moans, her back arching as I bury my face deeper between her legs.

"Shh," I whisper in warning. "You're going to wake Emily up, darlin'. I'd rather you come before that happens."

I look up and watch her nod fast with her lips pressed together, chuckling and getting back to work. I groan at the taste of her when my tongue pushes into her entrance, growing hard at the way she soaks my tongue. She's so ready for me that I can't bring myself to wait another moment. I sit up on my knees and slam into her in one smooth motion. Laura digs her face into the mattress, face contorted with pleasure when I start thrusting hard and fast. I never get tired of being inside of her. She's too goddamn sweet and addicting.

I lean over her and wrap my lips around her nipple, sucking while my cock works her. She locks her legs around my torso and lifts her hips up with every thrust to match my pace. At this point in our sex life, she knows exactly what I like and I know exactly what she likes. That's why both of us draw near climax all too soon. I can feel her start to tense up around me and I'm not fair behind at all, biting down on the bud while her nails claw down my back hard enough to break skin. I kiss my way up her neck until I take her lips between mine, my tongue fucking her mouth as hard as I fuck her. Laura moans when I reach between us to flick her clit and then her walls squeeze me as she comes.

I push my hips into hers, my cock twitching when I feel it pulse with the force of my own orgasm. Both of us groan, clawing at each other and kissing with greed as we finish off. God fucking damn, this never gets old.

When it's done both our bodies go limp. I pull out of her and lie down beside her, the two of us panting hard and trying to catch our breaths. Laura turns to hug my body and I kiss her forehead, dragging my hand down her back lazily. I enjoy the simple moment and how we have it all to ourselves. Life has been so busy I feel like I don't see my wife enough.

I officially retired from boxing one year ago. It became the biggest part of my life after leaving South Bloods behind. I took refuge in the sport and let it define me, found solace and meaning in it. I made the most of my years as a fighter. Everyone called me The Strike for a three-punch combination move I'd mastered during my career. I preferred it to Raze any day. I even used boxing as a way to propose to Laura a few months after we had Em. I proposed to her from the ring while she was there, sitting in the crowd, because that's how we first met. She seemed to appreciate it based on the way she jumped inside the ring and tackled the hell out of me, screaming yes.

The best parts of my life happened inside a ring and this past year without boxing has made me adrift with no real purpose. Luckily,

Laura is doing a lot better than I am. She opened up her own gallery a couple of years ago and though she's never sold out, I know that's just down the road somewhere. She's too talented.

"Are you okay?" She murmurs, playing with the scruff of my beard.

"Just thinking," I admit. "I don't know what comes next for me."

She props herself up on one elbow. "Well, what do you wish you could be doing? If it was anything in the world."

I hesitate a moment, not knowing how she'll take the answer. "I miss being a leader. Boxing was great but it didn't fulfill me the way being a leader did."

She nods thoughtfully but doesn't look surprised. "Well, maybe you could combine both. Boxing and leading."

"What do you mean?"

"What if you became a coach? You've always said training makes or breaks fighters and there's little to no fighters that impressed you during your career. So become a coach. Make fighters that you can be proud of, ones that understand the sport as well as you do."

My brows come together. Coaching? It's never really come to mind before. But I guess it wouldn't be completely out of my ballpark. I've always analyzed every fighter that I fought, thought of ways they could improve their fighting to make them formidable opponents, and found myself wishing I could give them tips so they'd put up a decent fight.

"I don't want to teach bratty kids, though. I'm tough as balls, dar-lin'. I'd only want to coach men that could handle my ass-kickings."

"So do that," She laughs. "Let aspiring fighters come to you when they're ready to be trained as professional fighters and help them go pro. Whip them into shape. You might even grow attached to them and find new men to take care of."

I snort. "What, take them in as my sons or some shit?"

"Why not? You may be a leader but you're a nurturer. You take care of people. These men might need you as more than a coach and you could be that for them too. Your leadership has no limits, babe. The world needs it."

"I don't know about that," I mutter but I can't deny that I'm starting to think about it. And the more I think about it the more appealing it sounds.

"Keep an open mind." Laura kisses my cheek. "What do I always say? We're meant to learn from the people around us. Coaching will be a whole new experience for you and open doors you've never visited. Maybe you'll find more soulmates down the line."

I shake my head with a smile. Laura's free-spirit has never once wavered in the years I've stood by her side. It's staggeringly different to my grounded one but she's the one who gives me courage to try new things.

"Okay," I agree softly. "I'll look into it. Marco coaches the Boston gym I own—Fighter's Den. I'll ask him if he's willing to let me give him a new position so I can take over."

"Coach Resnick." Laura wiggles her brows. "Hot."

I grab her by the waist and she squeals, bursting into a fit of laughter when I roll on top of her and kiss the hell out of her face.

To this day her smile makes my heart stop a beat. It's the same smile that changed my life and made me who I am.

"Let's get dressed." I peck her mouth when I hear shuffling down the hall. "I think we woke our daughter up."

"Dibs on the shower!" She kicks me off and jogs away, laughing when I smack her on the ass and watch her go.

I quickly pull on a pair of boxers, just making it time when Emily bursts in the room with a grin. She has the same smile as her mother. Same eyes too. Her hint of sass is my doing, however.

"Breakfast time!" She announces. Then she scrunches her nose. "You need more clothes, Daddy."

I laugh and look down at my state of undress. "Your father has an impressive figure. Let me show off, darlin'."

"Gross!" She pretends to throw up. I roll my eyes. So goddamn dramatic. "Let's go! Breakfast!"

I lean down and pick her up, throwing her over my shoulder. She squeals with laughter as I bound down the stairs lightening fast and pretend like I'm going to drop her. We're both red in the face by the time we make it to the kitchen.

Emily sits at the kitchen table colouring while I whip up some chocolate chip pancakes. I get a text as I flip one pancake over and read through it. It's Mitch.

As the years went by we were forced to drift apart. He works for my city business and went into safe-house guarding but he still has some active connections to South Bloods after volunteering to be one of the men to keep eyes on them. I may not lead them anymore and I never will again but the fear of putting my family danger is too persistent. It's better that I make sure I know what they're up to at all times and that no one brings my name up again.

South Bloods think I'm dead, after I made another deal with the leader of the Asesinos to spread a rumour about getting caught in a street killing last year, which is why I've had to distance myself from Mitch so our friendship can't be traced back to my family. He's a good man—he chooses to keep an eye on South Bloods for my sake even if our friendship is the cost. The text is nothing more than a status update and I respond with a simple enough message. Maybe one day down the road we can pick up our friendship where it left off again.

For now I have to stay under the radar. I started from scratch when we got to Boston, forging all kinds of records so there'd be no way to connect Raze and Greg together. It hasn't been easy. I have to lie my way out of a lot of things. Emily is growing older and sometimes she asks how her parents met. Laura and I told her the truth for the most part, that we met at one of my matches and I chased Laura down, but altered some details. I don't know that I'll ever tell her the truth about my past. I don't know if I'll ever tell anyone. I have no way of knowing if my past will truly stay past but...everyone has one, right?

"Daddy, you're going to burn the pancake!" Emily calls and I curse, flipping it over. It's slightly charred but edible enough, right?

"Make a new one." Laura appears by my side, snorting with laughter. I raise the spatula threateningly and she sticks her tongue out.

"Mama, look," Emily whispers excitedly, pointing at the kitchen window. "It's Daniel!"

"Who the fuck is Daniel?" I demand.

Laura smacks my arm. "Language. And Daniel is the boy she has a crush on. Lives across the street."

"Good. My gun happens to shoot that far."

Laura isn't even fazed. She's long since accepted I'm an overbearing father. "Oh, please. He's too nice for Emily."

"What does that mean?"

"Honey, the only male figure in her life is you and you ooze testosterone. That's the example she's growing up with so she's definitely going to end up with a hot-headed man that's the furthest thing from nice."

"And I'll kill him too."

"Wrong." She taps my nose. "Because deep down you're just like that so you're going to get along with him even if it's the last thing you want."

"And you happen to know all this how?"

"Because I'm always right, love." She stretches up on her toes to peck me.

I watch as she heads over to Emily and smothers her with kisses until they're both laughing too hard to catch their breaths. I can't help but watch my girls with a smile, knowing I'd be anywhere but here if it wasn't for them. And maybe I can't change my past or who I used to be but I can keep moving forward, keep learning new things, and keep helping others. A certain shy and sassy painter taught me that. We lock eyes and she winks like she knows what I'm thinking. I raise a brow right back because she really has no idea just how much she's changed my life.

As all soulmates should.

www.ingramcontent.com/pod-product-compliance
Lightning Source LLC
Chambersburg PA
CBHW071826190726
48292CB00005B/1632